M000202501

sunflowers in the afternoon

a novel

by

Sky Pelletier Waterpeace

Chapter 1

I fold the letter carefully and hold it while I close my eyes, tight. Images are flitting through my mind, rapid-fire, too many and too fast to process or think about... I'm breathing heavily and I pull in a loud, harsh breath. "Got to get a-hold of myself." I open my eyes suddenly, realizing I'd spoken out loud. I start to unfold the letter and stop, refold it again. I shake my head. I pick up the envelope from where it had fallen on the tabletop, and carefully slide the letter back in. I turn the envelope over so the writing is safely hidden on the underside and—*the photo!*—quickly pick up the photo from the table. I'm rushing, and I fumble; I've dropped the photo, right-side-up, on the floor. I start to say, "Dammit!" but long habit has suppressed the word even in this moment; what comes from my mouth is instead a stuttered "d" sound swallowed by a scowl. I lean over and pick up the photo. I close my eyes tightly again, but not fast enough; I feel hot tears squeezing out. I take in and let out a large breath of air, and open my eyes.

The eyes looking up at mine are smiling, both pairs—smiling out of the yellowish photograph. I blink to clear the tears from my eyes. I transfer the envelope to the hand holding the photograph, and dab at my face with the back of my free hand. I sniffle. I look into the eyes in the photograph, first hers, then mine, then hers for a long time.

"I hesitated to write you..."

I shake my head slightly and breathe again, another long breath, but this one more controlled than before. I look again at the two pairs of eyes—so smiling, so *young*—and slide the photograph in between the leaves of the letter, already inside the envelope. I worry suddenly *what if the photo falls out? what if* and glance quickly around; I see a hardcover book on the nearest shelf that's the right size. I open the book and place the envelope carefully inside. *Don't...* I open the closed book, and quickly, embarrassedly, remove the photo and stare at it again, this time clear-eyed. *So young. She looked so happy.* Although there is no one around, I glance around the empty room while sliding the photo back into the envelope and the envelope back into the book. I glance at the time on my watch and stifle another "damn"; I'm running late. I open the flap of my satchel, which *thank God* is unfastened still, and place the book safely inside. I quickly fasten the satchel, dart my eyes about until I spy my Stanley, and in one movement grab the Stanley and the satchel and am walking out the door, patting my pants pocket to feel the car key there. *I can read it again at the office.*

***

Karl is smiling at me; his eyes are twinkling. I glance up and catch him, and his smile expands into a grin. I squint at him, wondering how long he's been watching me. "What's up, man?"

Karl laughs, the sound bursting from him explosively, as though he'd been holding it back until then and, with my question, couldn't hold it back a moment longer. "What's up?" Another, smaller, laugh. "That's what I've been wanting to ask you." He smirks. "For about a hour."

He couldn't have been watching me for an hour. Could he have? I close my eyes momentarily, breathe deeply, and then fix my eyes on him in what I expect is a level stare. "What do you mean?"

3

Karl's face erupts in laughter again. He guffaws loudly and smacks the surface of the large oak table we share, hard. If the table weren't so heavy, so sturdy, my coffee cup probably would have jumped. I notice that it's nearly full, but I don't remember pouring a cup. I lift the cup to my mouth. The coffee is cold, room temperature. I glance at Karl. He's looking at me, grinning, eyes twinkling. "That's the other thing."

"What other thing?" I sip the coffee again. It's cold enough to be enjoyable on its own. *It's passed that no-man's-land lukewarm temp where you can taste how bitter it actually is. This is good. Smooth.* I finish the cup. "What other thing?" I repeat, crinkling my eyes a bit and smiling at him myself.

"The other thing." Karl comports himself and leans forward in mock seriousness. "Is the coffee."

"What about it?" *I think I know exactly what about it.*

"You know exactly what about it, don't you." It's not a question. His eyes are still smiling at me. "It's cold, right?" He smiles, and answers his own question, "Right." I mutter an affirmative sound and he continues gleefully. "The first thing was, that you haven't said a word in at least an hour. An —" he emphasizes the word, waving both hands briefly in front of his face—"hour. That—" another punctuating gesture—"my friend, *that* is *un*like you." Karl straightens himself up and looks me over briefly. "The coffee was just the, how do you say? The icing on the cake. The finishing touch."

"What about the coffee?" even though I know exactly what about it.

Karl snorts mirthfully. "You know exactly what. Man. You're funny." I realize I am fidgeting with my pen. "You poured that cup of coffee, what? Like, an hour ago? That tiny little Stanley cupful and you haven't finished it in over an hour. Hell, I don't think you even touched it." Karl leans over. "Tell me I'm wrong."

I smile. "No. When are you wrong?" He grins at me. "No, you're right. I don't even remember pouring it."

"O.K." Karl makes a show of resettling himself on his seat, and then places both hands on the oak table. "So," he begins with exaggerated concern in his voice, "what is it? What's troubling you?"

I'm looking at Karl and he begins to fade and change and *it's been almost twelve years. I haven't thought about her in probably at least five or six. Why now? Why am I* suddenly I realize that my vision is distorted, that my eyes have filled with tears, now dribbling hotly down my cheeks. I blink, and Karl has sat up suddenly and is looking at me intently. "Jesus man, seriously—are you O.K.?"

I wipe my eyes with the back of my hand, then mop the tears from my cheeks with my sleeve. I'm not crying really; the tears came on like a wave, a wave of warmth through my body and hot tears dribbling out, but my breathing is steady and I can feel my steady heartbeat in my ears.

"I'm O.K. I'm sorry. I was trying to—we've been working on the new protocol, and I—I wanted to focus. On that." *I could have told him right away, an hour ago. He's my best friend. He's not only my partner. He would have understood.* "I don't know. I should have—could have. I could have just told you, I guess." *He'll understand now. Tell him.*

6

"Tell me what? Jesus, man, what is it?" Karl is squinting at me.

My eyes are clear and I no longer hear my heartbeat in my ears. *Tell him. He'll probably know what to do.* "It's..." I take a deep breath. "I got a letter this morning. Like, in the mail. An actual letter."

"O.K...?" Karl is looking steadily at me, and I'm looking steadily at him.

"It was from Jane."

"Jesus Christ."

***

"Still," Karl says as he puts down his fork, "it could have been worse, right?"

I snort, not looking up from my plate of saag paneer. Karl hadn't said anything for only a few seconds after I'd told him earlier, before promptly suggesting that we hit up the Indian buffet for lunch. He then offered to drive, whether to entice me or to show off the mileage of the electric car he'd gotten before selling me his old one, I don't know. *I don't care. Karl is a good friend.*

"Seriously, it could have been worse. I mean there are hundreds of reasons she might have gotten in touch with you." I look up from my saag paneer; I can feel myself glaring. I quickly look back down, but not so quickly that Karl didn't catch the glare. "I mean, maybe not hundreds, but dozens.... I don't know, man, I'm just saying. It could have been worse."

I swallow and pat my lips with a napkin. "Anything, at any time, could be worse. Anything," I pause to firmly wipe my mouth *this stuff is greasier than I realized* before resuming, "could always be better, at any time. It's tautological."

"Yeah, yeah. Mr. Mathematician. Everything is tautological, right?"

"Right."

"So, like I said:" Karl pauses, waiting for me to look back up at him, and I do, pausing in my chewing, a half-bitten piece of paneer in my cheek. "It could have been worse."

I nod slowly, and swallow. "You're right." Karl winks at me, but I'm not in the mood. "No, but seriously. You're right. When you're right, you're right. And you're right."

"So..."

"So, I'm fine. I just want to focus on the new process right now, on the plans. I can worry what to do about—about the letter later."

"Well, I mean...." Karl looks at me intently. "I mean, you're going to call her, aren't you?"

I take a sip of water, deflecting. Karl leans back in his chair and looks steadily at me, his eyes cool. *He's always the level-headed one. Always the level-headed one. I'm the one who* "I'm going to—I don't know." I sip the water again; it's cool on my lips and tongue. "I haven't decided exactly what to do."

"Dude." Karl has leaned forward and his voice is low, conspiratorial. "I don't presume to tell you what's what..." I snort. "O.K., I love to tell you what's what, but you know what I mean." He pauses, then taps the table with a fingertip. "This is important. You *have* to call her. You have to." He straightens up slightly. "I mean you don't have to tell her—you don't have to tell her what we've been working on. But you've got to at least call her. Jesus," he leans back in his seat again, the conspiratorial tone gone. "At least let her know you got the letter."

"No, you're right. I'll call—I'm definitely going to call her." I breathe. I think I can hear the blood in my ears again. "I just don't know what to say..."

Karl laughs, ebulliently and loud. A couple at the table behind him and off to the side glance our way, and I squint at them. They turn back to their conversation. Karl's laugh was brief, and he leans back in, conspiratorial again. "We happen to have something for that, buddy." He taps the side of his head with his finger. "Let's finish up here and get back to the lab."

I smile. "O.K., but I'm getting another plate first. I mean, we're here now, right?" I wink at him and stand and start walking to the buffet.

Karl chuckles. "You got that right. We are here now, that's for damn sure." His voice fades behind me. The buffet trays sizzle and steam rises from the cracks around the edges of the trays.

Chapter 2

I'd planned to work on the new process when we got back to the office, but I was having a hard time concentrating. I'd eaten one too many plates of Indian buffet food, and my stomach felt like it was going to burst. It's almost two hours since lunch, and it's only now beginning to settle down. I haven't been able to concentrate on the plans, so I had laid in the hammock, reading. I wake up with a start. *I thought I was reading...* Karl is standing over me, over the hammock, smirking. "Stay up all night reading 'classics', right, but I try to give you something *useful* for our work, and *then* you get some sleep? Eh? Is that it?"

I belch, loudly. "Oh my. That felt good." The pressure has relieved in my stomach. I'm still very drowsy, but I feel much better. I feel *peaceful* like I can get some work done. "What time is it?"

"It's almost 15:30." Karl is still standing over me. "You've been asleep nearly two hours. Well, ninety minutes anyway." I lift myself up, or try to; I shimmy backwards in the hammock until I'm sitting up, more or less. "Once I realized how asleep you were —after forty-five minutes..."

"I appreciate that." *He knew I'd passed into delta-wave sleep, so he let me sleep for one full cycle. He knows me well enough to know my sleep cycles go thirty minutes or eighty-five. I must've fallen asleep right at I* glance at my watch. "15:25. I must have fallen asleep almost as soon as I laid down."

Karl smiles and turns away from the hammock. "I'm surprised you made it all the way to getting your head back. I think I heard you snoring." I can hear from his voice that he's smiling. *I always thought he was kidding about me snoring until I started hearing it myself.* "I made you some tea."

"Green?"

"No, oolong. Didn't you tell me—"

"Yes, that's right." I swing my legs over the side of the hammock and meet Karl as he brings me a quart-sized mug of oolong tea. "Green is only good—"

"—on an empty stomach. You think I only pay attention when you're talking about neurolinguistic programming. C'mon, man!"

"I only talk about NLP so much because you don't pay attention if I only mention something once." I smile just in time for Karl to punch my shoulder. "Ow!"

"*Maybe* if you didn't talk about NLP all the time, I wouldn't have to pay such careful attention to keep track of what you're on to each time."

"Touché." The tea is still too hot to drink, I discover after an exploratory sip. *Maybe I should* "Let's... um..."

Karl looks at me. His eyes are soft. I clench my jaw. There is a pause, just for a moment. "We can—"

"I was thinking—"

"—just go over the—"

"—maybe just—yeah. I mean, we—"

"—yeah." Karl stops. "You go." I sip my tea carefully. "No, go ahead." The tea is almost drinkable.

"I was going to say, I feel fine. We can keep going over the new protocols, or we can try out the prototype on my—" *I am not ready for that.* "We could—I mean, maybe it's better to just use the old protocol. The—the creativity one."

"You mean—for the—apply the creativity protocol to the new one?" Karl is being judicious.

"Yeah, I mean." *I'm being ridiculous.* "Look, I'm not—I don't want to think about the whole thing with Jane right now. I don't know, I think that carb-coma cleared me out. I feel fine. Let's try using the creativity protocol, and see if we can make some progress on that design of yours, for the new frequency modulation method."

Karl is looking at me. I look back, and sip my tea. It's bearable, but still very hot. *It's good. I always forget how much I love oolong tea.* "If you think—"

"Yeah, I think it'd be good for—I think it'd be good. Besides, I'd love to figure that circuit out."

"Figure it out before I do, you mean..." Karl's smiling.

I smile back. "That's exactly what I mean."

***

I'm lying on the waterbed, electrodes pasted to my temples and neck, headphones and electronic eyemask on. I'm being bathed in lights, sounds, and slight electrical jolts. Karl is somewhere, somewhere *somewhere. somewhere I have never travelled, gladly beyond* out of my hearing and sight, and electrically shielded from me, just in case. *I'm standing on the dock. It's early morning and there is mist on the water. It's cold. Jenny is with me. Jenny is right by the water. I walk towards her; she turns and smiles.*

I blink. Karl is looking at me, looking down at me from over the waterbed. He must have just removed the eye mask. "Hey." I'm clear-headed. I sit up.

"Hey. How was it? Anything good?"

"You were—no. I mean, nothing worth talking about right now. It's on the tape."

I frown. I'd been hoping that the microphone suspended overhead would have picked up me narrating something useful. *I must be more distracted than I*

15

remembered. What was I thinking about before I clicked out? Something about... "I didn't talk about... did I mention the plans at all?"

Karl frowns at me. "I think you were probably still—I think maybe you had stuff on your mind. Why don't you take the rest of the day off? We can debrief tomorrow."

"O.K., sure."

Karl helps me to disconnect the electrodes. He wipes everything down and puts away the equipment while I head over to the control room. "What are you doing?" he calls from behind the open lab door.

"I'm just downloading—" Karl's come into the control room. "I'm just copying the audio and the data files. I figure if I get a chance later I can review them. If nothing else, it'll help me fall asleep." I smile to Karl. He's frowning slightly.

"Look, man..." He walks over to the computer and puts his hand on my arm. "Just—just take the night off, O.K.? We can debrief tomorrow."

I turn and look at him. "What is it?"

16

Karl stares at me for a moment then scratches the back of his head. He turns away and sits down at the other end of the table. "Look. You were—you were talking about your sister. I couldn't make out a lot of what you were saying. I'll have to post-process it anyway. Let me take care of it, and we can debrief tomorrow, O.K.?"

Jenny.

I close my eyes. *Jenny is standing at the end of the dock. She turns and smiles to me. There's mist over the water. It's just past dawn.*

"O.K." I fidget, move towards the USB drive sticking out of the computer, then withdraw my hand and sit down in Karl's chair. He's sitting a few feet away from me, leaning back casually. "O.K."

"Look, it's probably nothing. A lot of it seemed garbled. I think we were just working through some stuff. After—you know. After the letter and everything."

"I'm sure you're right." I stand up suddenly, knocking the rolling chair backwards. It bangs against the metal table edge with a dull thump. "You're right. I'm going home."

"Good. I think that's good. Listen," he's stood up and is following me out of the lab. "I'll process this stuff, and if you want to listen to it tonight, I'll upload it to the shared folder. O.K.?"

"Sure, fine." I'm putting on my jacket in the work room. I've forgotten my Stanley somewhere. I turn around and Karl hands me the Stanley. I smile. "Thanks, man."

"I've got your back, dude." Karl claps me on the shoulder, firmly, kindly.

"Thank you." I put my free hand over his for a moment. "I appreciate you."

Karl laughs, a short staccatto. "Mutual, my friend. The feeling is mutual."

I walk outside. It's a bright and cold November afternoon—evening, in fact. After daylight savings time I guess. It's getting dark.

Chapter 3

Amy's home. "Hi..." She turns around quickly.

"Heyya!" Big smile. *Smells good.*

"You're home early...?" I put my bag down on one of the kitchen chairs. Amy's drying her hands on a small towel. "Did—did you cook?" I try to peer past her into the kitchen.

"Never you mind." She's smiling at me. *She's a sweetheart. I'm lucky to have her.* "I —well, I figured maybe you—that is..." she stammers to a halt.

I look at Amy steadily. "You saw the letter?" I shake my head. "Of course you saw the letter. You must've brought the mail in yesterday. I didn't see it until this morning."

"I know." Amy walks over, puts her hands on my shoulders. "I didn't want to say anything to you yesterday. I mean, I wanted to, but..." She bites her lip gently. *I know that look.* "I wasn't sure *what* to say."

I nod. She is gazing steadily at me. "Oh..." her voice trails off and she pulls me against her. I have to stoop slightly *I always forget how much shorter she is than* and I wrap my arms around her and cup her head against my shoulder. I suddenly realize she's sobbing. I try to pull back but she is wrapped tight around me. "Amy? What is it?"

Amy doesn't say anything; she just whimpers softly and then pulls back, shaking her head. She turns back into the kitchen. "I recognized the handwriting, even if she hadn't put her address on it." She adjusts a pot on the stove with a clash. "Sorry..." she glances over at me. "I guess I'm more upset than I realized. I was so worried about what you'd—how you'd feel..."

"It's O.K. Gosh, I'm sorry. I didn't even think—I wasn't even thinking—I was too, I guess." I walk next to Amy by the stove and brush a lank of hair behind her ear. "I'm sorry. I was all wrapped up in it. I wasn't even thinking how you'd—it didn't even occur to me." *Selfish.* I cup Amy's chin and pull it to face me. "Are *you* O.K.?"

20

"I'm fine. I'm fine!" She angles her chin away from me and half-shrugs, kind of wriggling the shoulder nearest to me. It's a dismissive gesture which I've seen hundreds of times. I close my eyes. "Hungry?"

I surprise myself by saying, "Actually, yes."

She's stirring something and gives me that sideways half-smile. *That didn't take long.* "You sound surprised."

"I am, actually. Karl—" I clear my throat.

"Karl, what?"

"Well. Karl actually—he took me out. For Indian food."

Amy turns to me suddenly. "No!" It's mock outrage, but I can't tell if she's actually upset at all.

"Yeah, I guess he was trying to, you know. Get my mind off things."

"You jerk. You went to Indian food *without me*?" *She's not really mad.*

I force a laugh. "Don't worry, I'll still eat whatever you're making! Don't want to waste this opportunity...." I poke at her arm.

"Oh, ha ha. Look, I work later—we're on different schedules...."

"Oh, honey, you don't have to—I didn't mean it like that." She's pouting, but *I think it's in good fun.*

"I just figure that if I don't take care of you, no one will. Silly me!" she slaps her forehead in a comically exaggerated way. "I forgot about Karl!"

I laugh and kiss the back of her head when I walk by. "I appreciate it."

She puts the pot down loudly and turns to me. "Do you? Do you really?" *Her eyes are shining.*

I stop and look at her. *She's tearing up.* "Of course I do. Honey..." She's launched herself into my arms and is sobbing again. I pet the back of her head. "It's O.K. It's O.K."

***

We've eaten, and we're sitting on the couch. "I'm sorry about earlier." Amy is looking at me.

"What are you sorry about?" *That didn't sound nice.* "I mean—it's O.K. You don't have to be sorry about anything." I wipe my mouth. "Also, thank you again for dinner. That was a treat."

"You're not just saying that to be nice? Were you even hungry?"

"Well, I wouldn't have been, if it didn't smell so good." I smile, and Amy smiles and stands up, takes my plate with hers and heads to the kitchen. I sip my tea and wait for her. "But really. I appreciate it. And *I'm* sorry, for not even—for not even thinking about how—about how it might bring things up for you."

Amy sits at the other end of the couch. "No, it's fine. I mean, Jesus. I know how much she meant to you." *I don't know if she means Jenny or Jane.* "We were never as close, you know." *Jenny.* "I mean, it's almost —no, I don't mean that."

"What?" She shakes her head. "What?" insistently.

"No, I was going to say... I don't mean it badly or, I don't know. I'll just say it, maybe it comes out sideways." *Definitely one of my lines.* "It's just—you guys were always so close, you know? And I don't know what it is—you'd think I'd be, I'd want to be anyway, closer to my sister. But it was like, you guys were twins, so you were automatically first for each other, and I was —I mean—fuck, I don't know what I'm saying." She looks at me and her brow furrows. "I guess I'm saying, what I'm *trying* to say, is just that I appreciate this. This, now. I appreciate that you and I can be close, and this other thing, Jane" *I can literally feel myself shudder even now hearing her name* "writing to you—you didn't even tell me what she was writing about? Anyway, I guess it just made me realize how much, how much happened, that led to this, to here. I mean, I've been living here for—almost a year, isn't it? I know we each do our own thing and you don't necessarily want your baby sister bugging you about everything and—"

I snort. "Why would you even say that? Don't you—I mean, do I give you the impression I don't like you living here?"

"No! No, not at all. I mean—"

"Because I love you being here. I love—I mean, I love that we have, not that we weren't close before, but—"

24

"No, it's true, I mean—exactly. That's exactly what I was trying to say, Jack. It's been really good to be able to be close to you, closer I mean, and I guess seeing her name, it just brought up all the stuff, you know, about Jenny—stuff I hadn't thought about in a while."

I nod. *I really have been being selfish. I was just thinking about me and Jane—and Jenny. I wasn't even thinking how Amy would feel.* "I'm sorry, honey. I realize—" I shake my head and look around the room. I pick up my tea cup and start to bring it to my mouth, but stop and rest it on my other hand in my lap. It's still warm but almost cool. "I realize that, I mean I guess you're right. I took it like it was my thing, like I didn't really think about how it all affected you. You were away and everything—" *Jesus I'm insensitive.* "Not that—I mean not that being away has anything to do with it."

"No, I understand." Amy bites her lip. "I mean, you're right. I was at school—Jesus, it was my first year in school, and then—then that." She swallows. I make a slight move and she does that half-shrug thing. "I did, though, Jack."

"Did what?"

"I did...hide. In school." She's looking at me, and I sip my tea. "You must know that."

"I guess so. I mean, I never really thought about it." *Of course I did; of course you did.* "Not like that, anyway. Not like you were hiding. I figured—c'mon, I mean I figured you were busy enough."

"Well, I mean I *was* busy, but—it was also— I mean, I purposefully, like, buried myself in work, I guess. I don't know. I needed something else to focus on."

"I know. I mean, I understand."

"You were dealing with everything with Jane" *it's like an electric shimmer that goes through my body, I can't tell if I am afraid or* "and I guess I just figured I'd just, you know, just bury myself in work. It worked," she smiles, "I mean I graduated with honors."

"Well, you dealt with it better than I did."

Amy flushes, her cheeks suddenly bright red. "No, I didn't—I didn't mean it like that!" She reaches a hand out, places it on my forearm. It's my left arm, and I want to take a sip of tea, but she's preventing me, but *don't be rude* I pat her hand with my free hand, and lift my arm to sip my tea quickly.

"I didn't take it like that. It's fine. I mean," I take a sip and slurp the cool tea loudly. "It's good we're talking about this. I don't know, we never really talked about it."

"Yeah, well. I guess, it's like you say— always a silver lining, right?" She pauses. "Hey, so.... what was the letter about, anyway? Why did she write to you?"

My tea is empty. I turn and set the mug down on the little table by the couch, and turn back to Amy. My mouth twitches.

"Jane has stage four cancer." Amy's mouth drops open. "She thinks she's going to die, and she wants to make amends."

"Wow." Amy straightens up. "I don't know what I was expecting, but I wasn't expecting that."

I snort. "You're telling me."

***

We both sat in silence for a few minutes. Finally, I got up to boil some more water for tea. Amy waited on the couch while I poured a cup, and when I came back to sit down, she was leaning forward a bit. She starts talking before I'm all the way sitting down.

"Are you going to write her back?" She catches herself. "Or call her? Did she give your her number?" Amy's eyes are wide.

I nod. "Yeah. She did. And yeah. I don't know what to say, but c'mon, I mean, what am I supposed to say? I kind of have to call her, right?" I hear myself. "Not that—I mean, I don't know. I forgave her a long time ago, I guess." I shake my head and move to pick up the mug of tea, but it's clearly still too hot.

"Does she—I mean, do you think—did she give you any indication that she knows what you do?"

"No, I don't think so. I mean, no. She didn't say anything about it."

"Hmm." Amy gets up and walks into the kitchen. I hold my mug and blow on the surface of the tea, watching the ripples. She walks back in and waits by the door. "Jack..." I turn to look at her, and she walks around in front of the couch and kneels in front of me. She takes the mug and puts it on the side table, and takes both my hands.

She's looking right into my eyes *God she looks like Jenny. except for the hair* "Jack, do you forgive me?"

I scrunch my forehead. "For what?"

Amy takes a deep breath and looks at me again. She's still holding my hands. "Do you forgive me for—for hating Jane?" *Oh god.* She takes a slow, shuddering breath. *Don't say it.* "For what she did to—for—for what happened to Jenna." *She must be more upset than she's letting on, if she's calling her Jenna. I can't tell her.*

I take Amy's head in my hands, my hands on either side; I brush her hair behind her ears and smooth it. "Amy, there's nothing to forgive. I don't—I never did—I don't blame you for how you felt." I pause. "I mean, I know, we know, I know you, we, we both know that it wasn't Jane's fault." She nods.

"I know, but I really hated her. I blamed her."

"*I know.*" *But it was my fault.*

Chapter 4

Jenny and I are running through a field. There are sunflowers everywhere. Jenny is ahead of me and I am chasing her through the field of knee-high sunflowers. We are laughing and sweating, and when I catch her we both collapse into a laughing, heaving, sweating, out-of-breath pile, nestled amongst the sunflowers. We are eight years old.

We have been having a picnic. Mama's in the house with the baby, and we've been sent outside to play. We spent the morning walking around and discussing things seriously and making jokes and poking each other and racing to the next tree. We discover a stream and stand it in thoughtfully, barefoot, watching the water move past our feet. We are both surprised how cold the water is. It's August. It's warm out, but the water is startlingly, brilliantly cold. We stand on the small rocks in the small stream and we stare down at our naked feet, and the water, the cold water, washes the thoughts away.

Now we are lying, breathing heavily, sunflowers bunched on either side of us, all around. The air is humid and has a clinging, sticky feel to it, but we don't notice the air. We don't notice anything except how Jenny's hair has tangled everywhere. She brushes it behind her ears and looks at me. Her eyes are blue. I'm suddenly very sleepy. It's been the best possible day. Jenny says something to me, but I'm sleepy and it's hot out and I'm not hearing her. I'm lying facing her, facing her tangled hair and her blue eyes, and the sunflowers and the heat make the air seem scratchy, and Jenny puts her hand on my shoulder. "What?" I ask, my voice suddenly laden with sleepiness.

"I said," she says quietly, intently, "do you think this is what it's like to be dead?"

I open my eyes, squint against the August sun. "What do you mean?" The sun is bright and my body is heavy and we are lying with sunflowers against our backs, and Jenny is holding my shoulder, and she closes her eyes and presses her head down against her arm. She mumbles something into her hair.

"What did you say?" I've closed my eyes again, and Jenny and her hair and her eyes and the sun and the scratchy air and the sunflowers and Mama in the house with the baby and the picnic and the cold, cold water of the stream are drifting away.

Jenny mumbles quietly, not a mumble, but a whisper, quiet, intent, full of all the air and the sun and the flowers and the picnic, full even of the baby in the house with Mama and the stream and the future. "I think this is what Heaven must be like..."

I kiss Jenny's forehead and we both fall asleep in the field of sunflowers, in August.

***

"If Amy finds out," I begin slowly, "I don't think she will ever—I don't think she will ever be able to look at me the same way." I pause and fiddle with the handle of my coffee cup. I shift the phone to the other side of the table, and press the earpiece more securely into my ear. "I don't know—"

The voice on the other end of the phone is speaking and I stop. "—she'd say anything." It's not a question.

"What? Sorry."

"No, it's fine. Sorry, I thought you were done. I was just saying, I seriously doubt she would say anything. I mean to Amy, but really to anyone."

"But you know—"

"Jack, you know as well as anyone—two things, actually. You know two things, as well as anyone, if not more so." I sip my tea. I've forgotten that it's chamomile, not oolong, and the taste surprises me. "You know better than anyone the kind of things that woman was capable of, back when you were married."

"Yeah, exactly. That's exactly what—"

"Hold on. I'm not finished."

"O.K." I take another sip of the chamomile tea. Now that I remember it's chamomile, I enjoy the light flowery taste. I enjoy the idea that it will help me sleep imminently.

"That's the problem. You lived through everything with her, so that's how you know her as. You've gone through, you've processed it, you've dealt with it, whatever. But a part of you still wants to think of her now as being the person you experienced her being when you were married to her."

"O.K., right. Sure." I've heard this whole conversation before.

"Now listen. Really, listen. Put down your coffee or whatever, your tea, and listen." Even though Steven can't see me, I smile as I set down my tea cup. "The other thing you know, at least as well as anyone else, is how people can change. Especially when they go though something significant. Right?"

"Yeah, I mean of course. That's pretty much —"

"Yes, I know. In your line of work I would expect you would know that better than most people. You deal specifically with people who want to change, who are going through something significant. So, it's the same thing."

I'm silent on my end of the phone. I had been twiddling with the handle of my teacup, but now I stop and lean forward over the table. I close my eyes and take a deep breath. "So, you're saying..."

"I'm not saying anything you don't already know. You know that." His voice is kind, softer now. "I'm not telling you because you need to know, because you already know.

I'm telling you because you, like me, are not so much a slow learner as you are a quick forgetter. I know because that's how I am: I'm not a slow learner, but I am a quick forgetter, and I can forget something that I've known already, for years. I can forget something that I know so well that I make good money telling it to other people." Steven pauses. "I need to hear this stuff myself, that's half of why I tell you. And I know you know that too."

"I know." I smile, and I can hear Steven giggle slightly, a short, fast, muffled guffaw.

"I know you know. So, you know that people can change. She said she has cancer, and it sounds pretty serious. I'm not saying it's impossible that she will pull some shit—of course that's possible. But I think it's more likely that she legitimately wants to clear her conscience. And you're not the only one she needs to get clear with, but you're the perfect one to go to." I can practically hear his grin.

"Well, that's the other thing. Because, I mean... she doesn't know what we do, I don't think. So do I tell her?"

"Why not?"

"Suppose she wants to go through the process?"

"Why wouldn't she?"

"Well, that's exactly it. She probably would. I mean, I wouldn't charge her or anything."

Steven snorts. "Good. That would be a whole other level."

"But I mean..." I trail off, and take a sip of my tea.

"What is it? I don't see anything wrong with her doing the process. It's what you do, and you are good at it. You and Karl have got something figured out, and it helps people."

"The thing is... Karl doesn't know... I mean, he knows about Jane, and he knows about Jenny, but he doesn't know—he doesn't know everything. He doesn't know the details."

There is silence on the other end of the phone. My earpiece hisses slightly. Steven takes a deep breath, the sound coming through as a soft buzzing or whooshing sound. "So Karl doesn't know the details. So it's not just about Amy. It's about Amy, too, but also Karl. You're concerned that Karl won't look at you the same?"

"No, I mean." I stop, and I can feel myself scrunching my brow. I release the tension in my forehead and take a deep breath. "I guess I am just—concerned doesn't seem like a strong enough word, but worried seems too strong."

"It's O.K. to be worried, Jack. Just because you specialize in relaxation or whatever, doesn't mean you can't yourself be worried about your own life. So you're worried that Karl might find out details or Amy might find out, and so you might lose your other sister or lose your partner." There is a pause. "Is that right?"

"Yeah, I guess so." *Lose my other sister. Jesus.*

"I'd say—well, it's like this:" Steven clears his throat. "Do you feel like the right thing to do is to call her? Call Jane, I mean?"

"Yeah. I mean, of course. What else could I do?"

"Well, you could ignore her letter and not call her."

"No, that doesn't seem—that seems completely wrong."

"O.K. So call her. Take it from there. What happens, happens."

I close my eyes and shake my head slightly. "What happens, happens."

"That's right. And what happened," he pauses for effect, "happened." Another pause. "We can't change the past, but we can change how we think about it."

"O.K."

"O.K.?"

"Yeah. O.K. I'll call her tomorrow. And just deal with things as they happen."

I imagine Steven smiling. "That's the ticket."

"O.K. Hey, thanks man."

"My pleasure. I love you, Jack."

"I love you too, man."

I press the button on my earpiece to disconnect the call, and remove the earpiece and set it on the table. I take the last swig of tea. It's cold and the chamomile tastes vaguely sweet.

Chapter 5

I'm at the office, sitting at the wide oak table that Karl and I share. I'd forgotten it was Sunday, and I was surprised that Karl wasn't here when I arrived. *It's just as well. This is something I need to do by myself.* Karl would be in the office every single day, so he has a rule for himself that he has to take one day off, no matter what. He doesn't observe any religion, but he feels that Sunday is somehow appropriate. He likes to joke, "The Lord rested on Sunday, and that's good enough for me!" I have never bothered pointing out that the Lord rested on Saturday, not Sunday. I'm not sure if it's one of his inside jokes with himself. *I'm stalling.*

The letter is open on the table, sitting next to the envelope. I've already reread it twice. *I don't know what I'm looking for. Clues? To what? To whether she's really...* The photo is underneath the letter. It's face-down underneath the letter; I put it face down as soon as it fell out of the envelope when I took the letter out. I take a deep breath and move the letter to the side, uncovering the photo. I close my eyes and rub my right eyelid, scratching at an itch that probably isn't there. *I'm stalling. I don't know if I should even look at it. What's the point?* I reach over and finger the edge of the photograph, sliding it back and forth slightly by the corner, twisting it ever so little on the surface of the table. The photo is old *how many years has it been? It's been twelve years now. Twelve years!* and the four corners are each pointing in a different direction, so that the photo, face-down, rotates on a convex point somewhere on its surface. *What if I scratch the image?* Without thought I pick up the photo and turn it over. I'm holding it in my hand. I'm looking at myself looking at me. I'm twelve years younger in the photograph. It's yellowed, not from age, but because the light where it was taken was dim, and it was not exposed properly, and so there wasn't enough light for the film. *An old film camera. She was probably the last person in the world to use a film camera.* I haven't seen this photo in at least ten years. I didn't even know it still existed. I glance over at the other pair of eyes and quickly shut my eyes, wincing. I lay the photo back on the table with my eyes still closed. I reach for my cell phone and absentmindedly put the two ear buds into my ears. I pick up the letter and scan it for her number.

I type Jane's number into my cell phone and pause; I set the phone down and stand up suddenly, walk out of the room and down the little hall to where the office kitchen is. I boil water in the electric kettle. *She could tell Amy. She could tell Karl. She'll have to tell Karl, if she goes through the process. What will Karl—I don't have to worry about Karl. It's Amy. If Amy finds out—what if Karl—I haven't told him, and yet he is my partner. We guide others through the process, yet I haven't done it with him. What if he thinks that I shouldn't be—what if he wants to dissolve the partnership? I never patented the process. He could take it and claim it and I couldn't say anything. He could ruin me. But if she's really dying of cancer and if I don't want to live with this hanging over me any more then all I can do is—*

I leave the water boiling in the kitchen and walk swiftly back to the work room, pick my cell phone up off the oak table. Jane's number is staring off the screen but I barely see it. I press the "dial" icon before I can think about it, and turn and sit on the edge of the table. My heart is pounding and I can feel pressure in my skull.

The phone rings once, twice. It's rung several times, and then there is a soft click. "Hi, this is Jane. Leave me a message and I'll call you back. O.K., bye!" The voicemail beeps and I'm silent for a moment.

"Jane. Hi. Hi, it's me. It's Jack. I'm—" *afraid you are going to ruin my life again* "—I'm calling to—that is, I'm returning your—well, I mean, I got your letter. That's what I'm trying to say. I got your letter, and I—gosh it's been a long time. I appreciate that you reached out to me. I'd been thinking about reaching out to you for a long time, but— listen, I'm sorry. I guess we can talk about this all later." *It's now or never.* I squeeze my eyes closed for a moment and inhale deeply; I say the digits of my phone number. Out of habit, I repeat them. "O.K. So I guess it's phone tag, and you're it." *I'm being an asshole.* I pause. "Jane.... I hope you call me back. It took a lot of courage for you to write to me, and—and I hope you call me back." I take a shuddering breath. "O.K. Bye-bye." I whirl around and collapse into my chair and press the button on the ear piece. The earbuds beep loudly to signify that the call has ended. My heart is

44

pounding and there is sweat beading on my forehead. I close my eyes.

***

I don't know how long I've been sitting on the chair with my eyes closed, but when my phone vibrates and the earbuds chime in my ears, I'm startled. It takes a moment to register what the sound is; it's rare that I am wearing my earbuds when my phone rings, and I'm not used to hearing the sound. The chiming in my ears is a silly repetitive noise, like the earbud version of an ice-cream truck jingle. After a moment my brain clicks into awareness and I touch the button on the earbud, activating the call. "Hello?"

"Jack?" *It's Jane.* "It's Jane."

I feel something in my chest, and I *fall into a vast vacuum space opening up between here and there opening like a cone between herenow and therethen so that my heart and my blood and* her *heart and* her _blood are both existing in the same space as each other, and _spread infinitely far apart. Emptiness in my chest exploding with tingly electric glittery pulsing heart beating and breathing loud loud louder loudly* breathe

45

out slowly. My body is shaking. "Hi." My voice sounds far away. "Hi, Jane."

"Jesus it's good to hear your voice." I have a strange feeling as though my knees have gone wobbly and I've just fallen into the chair that I have been sitting in the whole time.

"You too." *I have no idea what to say next.* "It's—it's good to hear your voice, too."

"I wasn't sure if you would call me."

I pause. "I wasn't sure if it was a good idea." I swallow. "God, that sounds terrible."

"No." I can almost hear her shaking her head. "No, I understand. I mean—gosh, it's been a long time, hasn't it?" *Either too long or not long enough.*

"It's been a long time, Jane. I guess—I mean, well, you said in your letter that—is that right? Did you say you wanted to—to get together?" Suddenly I have the strange feeling that I may have made this part up. *Get ahold of yourself. She's a person. It was all a long time ago.*

There is light laughter on the other end of the phone. "No, that's right. If you don't

46

mind," she adds quickly. "I just feel like—
God I mean there's so much to catch up on,
and it just doesn't seem—I don't know, I
guess it's a lot to ask, but I was hoping
maybe we could just get together for, you
know, for a cup of coffee or brunch or
something." She pauses. "Is that—I mean is
that alright with you?" *She's not saying the
rest of the sentence. "Is that alright with
you, or do you still blame me?*"

I pause longer than I intend to, and then I
worry that it's portentous. "No, that would
be great. I mean—" I take a deep breath.
"I'd like that; I'd like to, if you'd like to. If
it's alright with you. I think it would be
good for both of us."

"Yeah, I think so too. I think it's long
overdue." She quickly adds, "I mean, not
that—I just mean that it's been a long time,
and I think it may be good for both of us. I
know it would be—I think it would be good
for me. I hope it would be good for both of
us."

"No, you are right. It will be. Let's have
brunch." *Like two normal people.*

"I know a place but I'm not sure if it's still
there. I can check and text you, if that's

O.K., and then we can figure out what day and everything..?"

"That's fine. Text me when you know about the place. Honestly, we can go whereever you like."

I can hear her smile. "This is a place I think you would like. I'll let you know shortly. And Jack..."

"Yeah?"

There is silence on the phone for a moment. "Thanks. For calling. I'm really glad you did."

"Of course. I'll talk to you soon."

"O.K."

"O.K." There's a pause. "Jane?"

"Yeah?"

I don't know how to say this. "I don't know how to say this, and maybe I should wait until we meet in person, but—I don't know. I just wanted to say, that I think it was— very brave of you. To write to me." I clear my throat. "Not brave, but—I just think it was—I don't know what I'm trying to say..."

"It's O.K., Jack. I think I know what you mean. And thank you. I'll text you in just a few minutes, O.K.?"

"O.K. Bye-bye for now then."

"Bye-bye. For now."

Chapter 6

I didn't know what to do with myself at Jenny's viewing. I don't remember getting there or anything that happened before seeing Amy. I'm standing in the side room, and all of a sudden Amy is in front of me. "There you are!" She rushes towards me. "I've been looking all over..." and she is holding me, sobbing.

My arms are around her, and she is pressed tightly against me, and I am acutely aware of the pressure of her breasts on my chest. I feel a hot flush of shame and I want to pull away, but Amy is sobbing on my shoulder, so I keep my hands where they are, wrapped around her, and her breasts press against my chest and heave when she takes a huge heaving breath, and I can feel the burning flush spread down from my face and past my neck, exploding outward in my chest, pressed there and stimulated and shimmering all the way down my body, everywhere, past my hips and bouncing back off my feet up through my legs again, rejoining the explosive flush in my chest where Amy's breasts are still heaving. *I have got to—I have got to--what can I do?* Mercifully, Amy slowly slackens her grip around me and eases away; I loosen my arms around her, and now she is still leaning on my but the pressure is lessened and I *oh my God one more inch and I am free, please let me* pull away.

"Let me take a look at you." Amy looks up at me and I gaze into her eyes. I can feel my face burning and I am afraid she is going to say something.

"Oh, Jack..." *Here it comes. How does she know? Of course she knows. It must be written all over my face. No one else knows me as well as—Jane isn't here, and Jenny can't—Amy must be the one.* "Isn't it awful?" Her eyes are shining, pools of tears brimming and then spilling back over, and she is against me again, her shoulders shaking and my useless hands pressed against her back, against her shoulder blades, and her breasts are again heaving on my chest as she sobs. I can smell her hair. It smells like *sunflowers!* something familiar, and I realize that I am crying now too, silently, hot tears running down my face and into Amy's hair. *Damn her! If she hadn't* I squeeze my eyes closed hard and push the image out of my mind. I hear a sound and realize I have let out an audible sob.

Some time later, Amy and I are sitting on a nearby couch. After the initial cry, holding each other for what felt like an eternity but could only have been a minute or so, we are now sitting, talking, catching up, almost as though our sister is not lying dead in the next room over, except that our voices are somewhat subdued, an effect of the atmosphere of the funeral home.

"So school's been good. They're really good about—about this kind of thing. All my professors said to not worry about classes this week and everything, and next week is Spring Break, so I basically don't have to worry about anything school-related for like, I don't know, two weeks?" Amy smiles and puts her hand on mine. "My math skills are on hiatus I guess. Good thing, too, because Calculus was starting to get—I don't know, it's fine, but I could use the time. To catch up and everything. I just hope I don't get behind this week, I mean since there's still—"

"If you need help—"

"—new material. Oh, Jack, I mean—I—of course I thought about you, but—that's the last thing you have to worry about right now." Amy is looking at me, leaning over. She is sitting on the couch across from me, perched on the very edge of the couch, leaning over to hold my hand, which is in my lap. I notice that Amy is wearing a skin-tight black dress, and I notice that her breasts are fuller than I remembered, and *Jesus what the fuck is wrong with me* she is leaning over towards me. I take a deep breath and look up and away slightly. *Hopefully I look thoughtful and not like I'm looking away from her tits. Jesus.*

"Amy. Honey." I take her hand in both mine, and scootch forward on my sofa so that she doesn't have to lean so far forward. "If you need any help, of course I can help you. I mean, c'mon."

"I know, I know. I just—I know you're busy and everything, and now th—now everything. And—I heard from Mom—at Thanksgiving I guess? I mean..." Her voice trails off. *Jane.* She is looking at me, the question hanging in the air. I clear my throat, and Amy continues tentatively. "It's none of my business. But." She closes her eyes or looks down, I can't tell, and shakes her head slightly, then looks up sharply, piercingly, directly at me. "Jane's not here, is she?"

I gulp; it's audible to me, and suddenly I am aware of how quiet the funeral home anteroom is. There is soft music playing somewhere, but I feel as though I can hear the swish of dresses in the next room, and as though the sound of my gulp must have echoed off the walls in the small room we're in. *Say something.* I want to say something, but my mind is suddenly concerned with the saliva in my mouth. I don't remember it being there before and I can't tell but it seems like it's more saliva than is usually there. *Don't throw up. Jesus, fuck, don't throw up.* My mouth is filling with saliva and I clench my jaw and squeeze my eyes shut and swallow hard, two times, three.

I open my eyes and Amy is holding out a glass of water. "...some water?" She is standing right in front of me, her *hipbones at eye-level underneath that sheer black* hand pressing now the glass of water into mine. I take an automatic sip and feel the cool water going down my throat as I feel the cool perspiration on my forehead, and Amy's voice drifts in, saying, "...didn't look very well all of a sudden. Gosh, Jack, for a second I thought you were going to pass out." She touches my forehead, then again, this time dabbing with a tissue. "You're sweating. Are you O.K.?"

I take another swallow of the cool water, and the heat begins to leave my forehead. My limbs feel a vague shimmer, like if I could feel the heat mirage off of concrete in the summer, as though the flush from before had incubated and cooked and finally boiled and my flesh had become numb and was now coming back from being asleep, the pinpricks replaced with a vague vibration of post near-nausea. I've finished the water and I hand the glass back to Amy, who's sitting to my left. She turns completely around to place the glass on the end table on her other side and I close my eyes again. I'm leaning back in the sofa, and I open my eyes and look at Amy. "What did you say?"

"I said you looked like you were going to pass out. I said that you're sweating and you look like you're going to pass out. Well," she frowns slightly, "looked. You look a lot better now, actually."

I take a deep breath. "No." I force a smile. "I heard that part. I meant before. I just—

I'm not surprised I looked—I mean I felt real funny for a minute there." I stop talking and look around. No one else is in the room with us. There are several other chairs and another small sofa *love seat* in the room, despite it being a small room. *I wonder if everyone is deliberately leaving us alone, or if it's a coincidence.* "No, I meant before. A minute ago or whatever, before you gave me that glass of water." I look back over at Amy. "What did you say just a minute ago?"

Amy glances down at her hands, twisting in her lap. She looks up at me with her eyes, her face still pointing downward. "I said..." She lifts her chin suddenly and again is piercing me with those eyes. "Jane's not here, is she?"

I look into Amy's eyes. *She blames Jane for this.* I make a motion with my mouth. *She blames Jane for this.* "She..." Amy's eyes are looking directly into mine, and *I can tell she is trying to control her face* she looks *angry!* expectantly at me. *She blames Jane for this. If she blames Jane, then probably everyone—maybe everyone else does too.* I clear my throat. *Good. So do I.* "No. She said she—"

I close my eyes for a moment, but when I open them, Amy hasn't moved. Her lips are pressed slightly, and her hands have stopped twiddling in her lap, over her legs barely clad in thin black fabric, and her breasts filling out the top of her dress are no longer pressed against my chest or my mind, and Jenny's hands are also still, folded over her lap in her dress, and Jenny's eyes are closed and still, and Amy's eyes are open, and looking at me, but they are not looking through me. *She doesn't know I had anything to do with this, and she thinks Jane does, and I can't tell her that it's Jane's fault, and I don't have to.*

I swallow, and the soft music in the background is no longer loud, and the quiet talk and occasional laugh from the other room is just sounds of people in another room, and I'm looking at my baby sister staring at me, and I hear myself say, "Jane didn't want to come today. She said she didn't feel comfortable," and Amy nods slowly, as though I've just told her something that I didn't tell her but I hope that I did. And now it's not my fault.

Chapter 7

I set my brown leather shoulder bag down on the wide oak table with a soft thump. I hear something and turn around quickly; it's Karl, leaning in the doorway of our work room, gazing at me. "Hey."

"Hey, man. I didn't see that you were here yet."

"No, I just got here. Want me to put on some tea? Oh—" he stops himself. "I see you have your Stanley. Well, I'll put some water on; you can have it when you're ready."

"Thanks man." I follow Karl into the kitchen. He fills the electric kettle with the filtered water with a slowness, a deliberateness, that I recognize: he has something on his mind. "What's up, man?"

Karl glances up at me over the kettle. He stifles a small smile and clicks the kettle button on. He glances at me again as he carries the water filter pitcher over to the sink. His back to me now, at the sink, he finally replies. "I noticed you didn't—ah—you didn't download the audio file." He shuts off the water and turns, looks at me, leaning his back on the edge of the counter. "From the other day. The one I mentioned."

"Ah. Yeah." *Something about his eyes.* "I wasn't—I ended up talking to Amy when I got home—she'd made me dinner."

"That night?" Karl smirks and snorts simultaneously somehow. "After all that Indian food?"

I smile. "Yeah, my thoughts exactly. What can I say? It's not like she makes dinner that often. Usually she's not even home yet when I get home."

"Yeah, you went home early that day, remember?" *No, I didn't remember that. Why was Amy home at that time, if I was home early? She couldn't have been expecting me...* I shake my head. "No, actually I didn't remember. That's funny." *Something about his eyes. I can't tell if—I think he's hiding something.* "Anyway. She'd made me dinner. It hadn't occurred to me, but of course she must've seen the letter. I don't know." I walk next to Karl, facing the sink, pick up the now-heavy water filter pitcher, and return it to the fridge. I notice that there is not much sparkling water left in the fridge. I turn back to Karl. *His eyes—I think he's hiding something, but I don't think it's malicious.* "Anyway, after I didn't feel like downloading it the other day, then I figured I would just wait until—until today. Go over it with you, and all."

Karl nods. "Well," he says. He pauses. He looks at me, barely containing the smile that's bursting out from his eyes. "It's just as well."

"What's that?"

"That you weren't in the mood." He smiles openly now, pleased with himself. "I didn't actually upload it for you." I squint at him a bit. I don't get the joke.

"You didn't upload it?"

"No."

I pause. I'm leaning on the fridge, and Karl is leaning on the counter. I hear the kettle start to make its whispering whooshing noise, indicating that the water is starting to heat up but is nowhere near ready yet. "So why—how did you—"

"Well, I—"

"Did you check the logs?" I can feel myself frowning, my eyes crinkled up, squinting at Karl as though to resolve with my vision my confusion at his actions.

"No." Karl is still smiling, and his lips twitch momentarily, as though he is about to burst out laughing but is trying to contain it. *I guess he thinks this is pretty funny. I'm not sure what's so funny, though.* "I just didn't —I mean, I didn't mean anything by it. Relax, man."

I close my eyes and take a breath and focusfully release the tension in my forehead and around my eyes. "Yeah, sorry. I'm—I talked to Jane yesterday."

Karl steps forward from the counter swiftly. "You talked to her? Yesterday? Did you see her?"

"No, we only talked for a minute." Karl eases back against the counter. He is watching me intently; the smiling shine in his eyes is gone. "We're going to get together. Meet up. Like brunch or something."

Karl nods. "Yeah." We are both quiet for a moment. "Hey, Jack. That's great. I mean, I think that could be really good. For both of you."

I nod quickly. *I am not sure I agree, but I'm nodding.* There is another pause. "But—"

"Yeah, sorry man. I mean, I'm not trying to —I just thought it would be better if—if we went over it together." Karl looks at me, his eyes soft. "You seemed pretty upset the other day, and I figured—just trying to help. I have the file ready, I just didn't upload it. And—" the smile is back. "You didn't log on to get it. Which I know—" he is very satisfied with himself, "not because I checked the logs, but because if you *had* gone on the server to download it, and it wasn't there, I'm sure I would have heard from you, wondering where it was. Since I didn't—" he is now smiling triumphantly, "I deduced—rightly, I presume? At least from the way it sounds... I deduced that you had not actually tried to download it. So," he has almost a flourish in his voice, "I was right to not upload it."

I am staring at Karl. He is smiling. *Proud of himself.* "O.K." I hear the kettle click itself off; the tea water is hot. I walk past Karl to the cabinet and remove two teabags and the tin of powdered organic cacao powder. I stop and look sideways at Karl. He's still leaning on the counter, only two feet away, his head turned and torso partially turned, watching me. "I don't get it."

"What?"

I squint at him again and turn around, looking for my teacup. "Have you seen—"

"The big one you use for tea is on the big table. No, excuse me. It's in the cabinet. He turns and opens the cabinet and reaches in. "Here, and here's that green one you always use for the cocoa." He hands me both mugs, and I look at him. "I ran the dishwasher after you left the other day." I stare at him. "I had nervous energy after—you know, after everything." I'm still staring at him. "What?"

"We have a dishwasher?"

Karl laughs and claps me on the shoulder with two hands in rapid succession. "You're a riot. Yeah." He briefly rubs my shoulders, at the base of my neck. "Yeah, we have a dishwasher. And it works, too. Look how clean that mug is. You probably didn't even know it was white on the inside."

I glance down at the quart mug I use for tea. Sure enough, the months' worth of brown and tan lines of tea stains are gone, and the inside of the mug is gleaming white ceramic. I glance up quickly. "Did you—"

"Don't worry, I used everything-free good-for-the-next-hundred-years hippy soap. There won't be any residue of anything that's not thoroughly vegan and certified fair-trade and organic. Jesus." This last word is said smiling.

I smile to Karl and put the two tea bags in the mug. I retrieve a spoon from the drawer and haphazardly pour two heaping spoonfuls of cacao powder into the green mug, and fill both with hot water. "Thanks man."

"Yeah. You're welcome."

"So." I stir the cacao in the water. "So what was so funny?" I turn to face Karl. "Before. With the—with the upload?"

Karl smiles. He shakes his head slightly and waves his hands in front of his torso in a wavering gesture. "I don't know man." He takes a step towards me and puts a hand on my shoulder again. "I guess I'm just trying to keep things light. I wasn't sure what kind of mood you'd be in." The corners of his mouth twitch. "But I knew one thing." Twitch.

"What's that?"

"I knew," Karl pauses and squeezes my shoulder slightly. "I knew that you hadn't logged on to retrieve the file that I made a point to process for you and then made another point to not upload for you." Karl's cheeks are lifted in a smile but his lips are pressed together, like he's holding back laughing in my face.

I stare at him. "You..." He bursts out laughing and turns away and walks nearly out of the room. He stops at the door and turns around. "Karl."

"Yeah?"

"Sometimes I think that you are the insane one."

Karl leans his head back and guffaws loudly, then wags his finger at me. "No, sir!" He shakes his head and wags his hand. "No, sir, I am the rational one. We decided that a long time ago. You are the crazy mathematician, and I am the sane and orderly computer scientist." He wags his finger furiously, smiling. "Get it right!" He is laughing.

I shake my head and stir my cacao. Karl is still chuckling as he walks down the little hall to the work room with the oak desk. I follow him, but he walks past the work room, headed towards the control room with the audio equipment. He has his hand raised above his head in a "follow me" gesture. I follow him, and by the time we are both sitting in the large comfortable chairs in the control room, he is no longer laughing. He is no longer smiling. "Listen..."

"What is it?" *O.K. this is what he's been getting at.*

"Jack..."

"Yeah?" Karl is looking at me. *I can't tell what he's thinking right now.*

"I don't know how to say this..."

"Just say it." I can feel myself squinting at him.

Karl closes his eyes and takes a slow breath. When he opens his eyes, he is looking directly into mine. "Jack..." he pauses. "I'm worried about you."

This time I laugh, suddenly, uproariously. Karl smiles. I've thrown my head back against the cushioned leather of the comfortable chair, and my hand, still holding the heavy green mug with the hot cacao (organic, fair-trade certified) is shaking, so that I delicately set the green mug on the control room table, in front of the equipment, so that I don't spill it. I take a deep breath and look at Karl. "You're worried about me? No shit?"

Karl smiles. "Yeah."

"That's what you didn't know how to say?" We are both smiling. "Well. No shit."

"No shit."

After we listened to the tape, I realized that he was serious.

Chapter 8

I remove the oversized studio headphones slowly, dazedly, and set them on the counter in the free space in front of the equipment. I close my eyes. I can feel my heart thumping in my chest. *I didn't say anything. Not really.* I take a shuddering, slow breath, trying to slow my thumping heartbeat. *I didn't say anything specific.* I take another breath. Karl's voice is piercing; though soft, it startles me. "Jack..." I take another deep breath and open my eyes. The light is dim in the control room—we usually prefer to keep it dim, lit mostly by the computer screens and the other instruments—but it seem abnormally bright for a moment. "Jack..." His voice trails off. I turn and look at him. He's leaning casually back in the big leather office chair, deliberately casual.

"Yeah?"

Karl starts to sit up in the chair, then settles back into it again. He crosses his legs—starts to cross them, then uncrosses them. He runs his hand over his close-cropped thinning hair. "Jack. You alright?"

I don't know. I know what I was talking about, but I don't know if you know what I was talking about. I make a sound in my throat that's less than a full word, somewhat more than a grunt.

Karl smirks. "Yeah, about what I... I mean—you can see why I was worried." He leans forward in the large seat, suddenly, and the chair swivels with the sharp motion, so that he catches himself on the edge of the table, steadying the chair. "Jack—Jesus, Jack, you...." Karl stops, shakes his head slightly. "Look, I mean, it's not really any of my business, right?" He's holding his hand out, palm up. I'm staring at him. *How much did I say? I need to listen to it again. I don't think I said anything specific...* "Look, I couldn't make out most of what you were saying—" *oh thank God* "—but from the sound of it—from the sound of it..." Karl is leaning towards me, his normally grinning face serious. "Jesus, Jack—it sounds like you blame yourself for—for what happened to your sister."

I realize I have been holding my breath, and I let it out slowly. It's louder than I thought it would be in the sudden silence. I close my eyes. Karl's words filter in. I don't know what he was just saying, but I hear, "...again. So I just—I just figured I'd play it for you, and if you want to talk to me about it, we can talk, and if you don't want to, then we—I mean, you don't have to talk to me about it, but if you think.... I mean..." Karl shakes his head. *He's upset. He's not angry, I don't think.* Karl looks at me suddenly. "I mean, Jesus man. How long have you been carrying this around?"

I move my mouth to speak, and my mouth is dry. I reach for the green mug of hot cacao. It's only lukewarm, and the thick drink does nothing to moisten my mouth. I swallow. "Look..."

Karl holds up both his hands. "Jack—you don't have to say anything. If you want to go through the process, we can do that. If you want to just talk about it, as friends... maybe you want to think it over..." He scoots his chair a little closer to mine. "I just wanted you to know—wanted you to hear—what was on the tape." He's looking at me. "I just wanted you to know that I was worried about you, and that if you want to talk about it, we can. But if you don't want to, that's fine. But—" he cocks his head at

71

an angle, looks at me with one eye forward. "But you might want to consider that—that there may be" the corners of his mouth crinkle up "there just may be a benefit to getting this shit off your chest." He's smiling at me now.

"Asshole." He grins back at me. I laugh, abortively.

"Hey—" he claps his hand on my leg. "It's what I'm here for, right? To bug you into being the fullness of your self, eh? I'm the sand bringing out the pearl of your genius, remember?"

"Yeah, yeah, yeah. Whoever said that was an asshole, too." Karl looks at me, opens his mouth, but I cut him off. "And I know—I know. I'm the one who said it."

Karl smiles. "Took the words right out of my mouth." He scoots his chair back to in front of his keyboard and clicks a few things on the screen. "O.K. It's uploaded for you, if you decide you want to bother with it." He's grinning at the screen. *At least I didn't say anything intelligible enough to incriminate me.* Karl turns towards me. *At least, not that he's letting on.* "So..."

"So..."

"When are you, ah—when are you going to —to meet Jane?"

I take in a breath and let out a noise with my exhale. "Shit. I don't know. I think we said today actually." I glance at my watch. "I guess it'll be a late brunch."

Karl glances at me. "Um, Jack?"

I stand up. "What's that?"

Karl stands up and hands me the empty green mug. "I think they call that lunch, dude."

"Yeah, yeah." I walk to the door of the control room and stop, turn around. "Hey. Karl."

"Yeah?" He's sitting back down.

"I just—I appreciate what you said." I gulp. "I guess I didn't realize—I guess I didn't realize I had so much—" I shake my head. "I guess I have some things to—to address." Karl is watching me. "I just appreciate what you said. I'm not trying to hide anything from you." *Except for what actually happened.* "I'm just—"

"I get it, man." He's standing up now. "I get it. She was your twin sister. I know how close you two were. I mean, it's got to be hard. Of course you blame yourself. It's perfectly natural."

"It's not that." I take a deep breath, then look at my watch. "Shit, I'd better get going. Look—" I stop. *I have no idea what to say to him right now.* "Wish me luck..."

Karl smiles. "Jesus, man. Good luck." He stops smiling. "Seriously."

I nod and walk out. I put the mug in the kitchen and head outside. It's much brighter out than I expected.

***

It's nearly 11:45 by the time I get to the diner. It's some little place Jane told me about. We were originally going to meet at ten I think, but I had texted to tell her something came up and could we delay it a bit. She texted back almost immediately that that was perfect, that she was running late anyway and would I mind if we made it an early lunch instead of a late breakfast. *Typical Jane. Gonna be late to her own funeral.* I suddenly remember what she said in her letter, about her diagnosis, and I'm disgusted with myself for thinking that.

I enter the diner and glance around. It's a small place, only about a half dozen regular size tables, and a few two-tops. Either it's not a very popular place, or the lunch rush hasn't really arrived yet. I check my watch; 11:37. No sign of Jane, but then I'm early. I hold two fingers up to the man who comes to meet me at the front *manager, probably —didn't say a word to me* and he leads me to one of the empty tables. *Towards the back, thankfully.* I sit facing the door and order a cup of coffee.

While waiting for the coffee, I close my eyes and try to remember the recording Karl just played for me less than an hour ago. It always surprises me when I don't remember things that I'd said in meditation. It always seemed like I ought to remember everything, even though I know that in an altered state of mind, one's state of mind is, by definition, altered. Nevertheless, it surprises me every time it happens. *Not that it happens all the time. This was a special case.* I'd clearly been thinking about Jenny, after hearing from Jane.

Jenny's standing on the dock, facing the water. I call to her, and she turns and smiles. She reaches out and takes my hands and fluidly, in a single motion, wraps her arms around me. Jenny and I are one person, flowing together, one energy in two bodies. I can't tell where hers ends and mine begins, or where mine ends and hers begins. We're bathed in sunlight that's coming from the sun and from the energetic connection between us. I feel lighter and lighter; I have the feeling that I'm holding her and that I'm one with her and that we're gazing in each others' eyes, eternally. I smell sunflowers. Jenny's eyes are locked on mine, we're holding hands and we're asleep in the field of sunflowers and we're standing in the sun on the dock by the lake house and we're—

"Jack?" Jenny pulls away and looks at me. "Jack?"

I open my eyes. Jane is sliding into the booth in front of me. I feel a sharp crack of adrenaline whip through my body. I start to move and Jane waves a hand at me. "I'm sorry. I was—"

"I didn't mean to startle you..." Jane looks at me across the table, and *I can still see her eyes looking at me, right after Jane called us. I can still see the look in her eyes* before she can say anything I wave for the waitress.

"It's O.K. I was just thinking." I take a deep breath. "Jesus, it's been a long time."

"Yeah." We look at each other. "You look great." She says this flatly. *I don't know if she's just being polite or what.*

"So do you." I force a smile. "Really—you look—I mean—"

"Better than you expected?" Jane smiles.

"I didn't mean it like that." I shake my head. "I don't know what I was expecting."

"Well..." The waitress cuts Jane off.

"Something to drink?"

***

We end up talking for nearly two hours. We eat, and we talk, and then after we're through eating we go outside and sit by Jane's car for another hour. She was in two hour parking, so she feeds the meter, and we sit on the steps a little ways away, and talk. It's nice. It's natural. I realize that I missed this. I can't think of how long it had been since we just talked.

Neither of us mentions Jenny. She only mentioned the cancer once, early on. She said that she'd share all the "gritty details" but that right now it was just nice to catch up. It *was* nice to catch up.

I found myself getting aroused after she mentioned that she was not seeing anyone. *God, she is just as attractive as she ever was.* I want to squeeze my eyes closed and turn off the images I see, but I can't, because I'm too busy chatting, talking about things. When it's been two hours and we see a parking cop up the road, we agree that we should cut it short, but that we should get together again later in the week.

I hug Jane goodbye, and I can feel her hips pressed against my crotch. I close my eyes and I can't stop what I see. I think she's deliberately pressing her hips against me. I pull back, my head, not my waist. We're still holding each other. Jane is looking at me. "Are you free tomorrow?"

Chapter 9

I'm sitting in my car, eyes closed for a moment, thoughts racing. I'm thinking about Jane, about her hips pressed against me, about the ways she was looking at me during lunch or brunch or whatever meal we just had. I'm thinking about how she mentioned that she's not seeing anyone and *how long has it been?* how I mentioned that I wasn't seeing anyone. I'm thinking *not about Jenny for now* that maybe I should have said something, suggested something. I know that it's not a good idea, and yet being with Jane, not talking about anything in particular, just talking, the conversation meandering as it always did with her, going on and on and able to go on and on indefinitely—I squeeze my already closed eyes harder closed. *I should have said something.*

My phone buzzes, and it startles me. I instinctively flinch, the whole side of my body shimmering in a single motion, reacting. It buzzes only once—a text message, not a phone call. I am frustrated that my reverie has been interrupted and pull my phone out of my pocket to see who I can mentally blame.

It's Jane.

The message is short. It's only three words. I stare at them and I feel as though my insides have sucked backwards and downwards and out somehow, not a nauseating feeling, and not a sinking feeling—not a bad feeling at all—just a sudden feeling of surprising vacuousness, profound emptiness without any negative "empty" feeling, just a space in which my body isn't there but I am just floating somehow. My mind is floating and my body is absent and I'm holding the phone and the car and my clothes and my body slowly reform around me, staring at the phone. Three words. I haven't moved, and then I'm moving. I've started the car (silently) and checked for traffic and am pulling out, I'm driving around the block steadily, quickly— I'm driving the speed limit and I'm being careful and I'm going as fast as I possibly can, my body suddenly afraid that something will be wrong. I slam to a stop at a red light and realize I hadn't texted back. I quickly retrieve my phone from my lap, trying not to fumble in the few seconds I have before the light turns green. Her message is still on the screen: "Follow me home?"

I quickly type out, "yes", hit send, and then, quickly, "omw"; I'm hitting send on the second message as the light turns green and I ease the car forward. I see the stairs where Jane and I had just been sitting for an hour, I see where we stood and she dug her hip against my crotch, and I pull up slightly behind where her car is mercifully still parked, blinker on, and honk. She glances back, sees me, and pulls her car out into the lane in front of me. I follow her.

I have no idea where she lives, and so I meticulously follow her. I'm thinking about the last time we had sex.

We'd been sitting on the couch, having a real state of the union type conversation. We had said the difficult things and had talked. The conversation had been tough to have, but we weren't angry with each other. We'd both agreed that it wasn't working, that *we* weren't working, and that the most sensible thing to do would be to call a spade a spade. We sat in silence for what could have been a while but in my memory seemed to be only a few seconds, and Jane looked up at me and said, "So, do you want to go upstairs?" She meant, did I want to go upstairs and have sex with her one last time, since we'd just decided that we'd broken up.

"Sure." I said. The rest of that afternoon was a blur, but I remembered that we did it at least twice, and that we were up there for a while. We probably napped in between. It was a while ago and I haven't thought about it in a long time, but it didn't turn out to be the last time we got together in that way. We continued to get together about once every week or so for another little while, even after she'd moved out. Finally, we somehow managed to knock it off, and started to actually begin to be truly separated, so our last "one more time" became our actual last time.

"Until today," I find myself saying out loud. Jane has just passed someone on the highway, and I anxiously check the range on my car. *Good thing it was fully charged this morning.* She drove when someone was following her the same way she drove when no one was following her, as though she were being chased. By the time I pass the car she'd passed, she's two cars ahead and I can barely see the back of her car. My heart is racing. I'm anxious and horny and *guilty* not sure that what we're about to do —I *am* sure, and I am sure it's not a good idea, but I am caught up in the chase, chasing Jane down the highway just like I chased her upstairs so many times after we'd decided that we *weren't good for each other.*

Mercifully, Jane pulls off the highway and almost immediately into a small developed residential area. I am not paying any attention to where I am. The houses look old, but not as old as the houses in the area where I live. The sun has gone in during the drive, and it's grey out by the time we pull up to her house, a little one-story. Stepping out of the car, I'm chilly. Jane scampers back over to me, her eyes shining. She's smiling, a big, free smile, freer than I'd seen all morning. She grabs the collar of my shirt and pulls me towards her and kisses me.

My mind goes blank.

Chapter 10

When, finally, Jane and I withdraw from kissing each other, my mind is no longer blank, but it's not thinking anything coherent either. I'm thinking about the feel of her lips and *her tongue* how her ass felt when I slid my hands down her back after *her tongue, moving against mine* wrapping our arms around each other in one motion *writhing, hungry* with our lips still firmly pressed against each other's. Jane is looking into my eyes, and I'm looking into hers. My mouth is wet. I clear my throat. "Bet you weren't expecting that, huh?"

I shake my head no. I swallow. "That was—good."

She's still smiling at me. "As good as you remember?" *She's teasing me.* I nod. "Good." She turns and starts walking towards the front door. She glances over her shoulder, "Come on!" with a little "come on" wave of her hand towards me.

I haven't moved yet. "Jane?"

She turns and looks towards me directly. "What?" She pauses briefly. I think she has a look of concern pass over her face, but maybe I'm imagining it. "What is it?"

"It's..." I don't know why I'm suddenly so nervous. "This may sound kind of funny, but —do you have..." I clear my throat again. She's looking at me with a quizzical look. I chuckle, suddenly realizing how odd I'm being. I smile. "Do you happen to know whether you have an outside electrical outlet? And, if you do, do you mind if I plug my car in?" Jane is staring at me, expressionless. "It's electric," I add.

"You wanna plug your car in?" She squints at me. "Right now?"

I hold up my hand, smiling. "No, frankly I *don't* particularly want to plug in my car, *right* this minute. Right *now* I really want to follow your little ass up those steps and into your house." Jane closes her eyes demurely for a moment, and a smile slowly creeps across her face as she opens them and looks at me. "It's just that—it's an electric car, and—it's entirely electric. It's not a hybrid." She's squinting at me but still smiling. I stammer on. "There's no gasoline backup, so if I run out of electricity, I'm

86

stuck. So," I gesture towards the car noncommitally. "If I can plug in while I'm here, then I won't—then I'll—"

"You'll have enough juice to get home?" Jane is smiling. *She's teasing me.*

"Yeah, exactly." I smile. "So—I mean, I don't want to run out on the way home, it's not good."

"I'll bet." She's just watching me.

"So...."

"What?"

I look at her. *She has this weird streak.* "I mean—well, do you have an outlet?"

She's no longer smiling; her face is neutral. "I'm not sure..."

I can see an outlet on the side of the house. I cock my head at her. "If you have one—would you mind if I plug in?"

Jane walks back towards me, slowly. "*If* I have an outlet, and I let you—" she pauses, a few feet away from me, and moves her mouth very deliberately, "*plug in...* How long do you want to—" she steps towards me, slowly, deliberately, "*plug in...*?"

I open my mouth slightly. She's only a foot away from me now; I'm looking slightly down at her. She licks her lips, slightly. *I don't think that was deliberate. I'm not sure.* I can feel my genitals beginning to swell with blood. "Actually..." I've lowered my voice conspiratorially.

"Mmm-hmmm?" Jane sidles up to me and hooks a finger in the hem of my jeans. Her finger is inside my boxers, against my skin, inches away from my growing erection.

"Well, actually... your house was a bit farther than I realized."

"Oh?" She bats her eyes at me in mock innocence. "Is that a problem?" She now how several fingers inside the hem of my boxers, on my hip.

"Well..." I put my hand on her forearm and my other hand on her opposite upper arm, holding her close to me. "It's just that, charging on a 110 volt outlet is kind of slow...."

"Is that right?" She steps against me, simultaneously pulling me towards her with her three fingers, pulling me against her by the hem of my boxer-briefs. "So what?"

"So..." I slide my hand down from her upper arm, in between her arm and her side, and pull her against me with my hand in the small of her back. She reverses her hand in my hem. I feel wetness leaking out of my semi-erect member. I'm pressing her against me, and she pivots slightly away on the side her hand is on, to maneuver her hand deeper inside my underwear. I close my eyes. There's electric shocks going up and down my body, emanating from where her fingers are sliding slowly down inside.

"Hey!" She hooks her free hand in my collar and gives me that squinty look, her lips slightly open. "I said, 'So what?' "

Holding her forearm still, I press it down, forcing her fingers to slide faster down. She wriggles her hand back so the backs of her fingers are grazing my skin. *I can feel her ring, scraping me slightly.* She pretends to resist, but lets me press her hand down until her fingertips reach my cock. She inhales slightly, suddenly, and wraps her hand around it. She licks her lips again. I cock my chin at her, and say in a low, breathy voice. "So I'll probably have to be *plugged in*—" she squeezes me; I'm as erect as I can get in the confines of my jeans, and her hand doesn't fit all the way around. "—

for, well—" she's holding me firmly now, her lips parted, her eyes staring at my lips. "—probably a few hours." Her eyes get wide and she looks at me. She licks her lips.

"Is that right?" She tugs softly on my cock.

I nod. "A couple hours—" I slide my hand down to her ass again, and pull her harder against me, pressing her hand, wrapped around my swollen member, hard against her. "—at *least*."

I lean down to kiss her and she jerks her head away suddenly. I take my hand from her forearm and brush it lightly across her hair, and then grab a fistful of her hair, in the back. Her mouth is open and her eyes are wide and she's staring at me in mock horror. I pull her face to mine and she pretends to shake her head a bit and then her lips touch mine and her mouth explodes against mine, her tongue in my mouth, her hand squeezing, pressed between us by my hand pulling her by the ass against me, my other hand still holding a clump of her hair, moving her head with it slightly while we kiss. She's making a deep, almost wailing, moaning sound. The wetness oozing out of me is leaking freely over her hand.

90

After a moment, I loosen my grip on her hair. She continues kissing me, then pulls back her head abruptly.

"In that case—" she gives me a quick peck on my lips and withdraws her grip on my member, withdrawing her hand almost completely, pausing with her fingertips just inside the hem of my underwear. "—you can plug in." She gives me a look. "For several hours." The corners of her mouth twitch. "As long as you have enough juice..." She pulls away suddenly and walks towards the house. She points to the side of the house without stopping as she scampers up the stairs to the porch. "The outlet's over there. I'll be inside. Hurry up."

I lick my lips. She's at the door, turned around looking at me. "Don't worry." I smile. "I'll be right in."

"Good!" she says lightly, and disappears into the house.

***

Jane and I fall asleep holding each other, and when I wake up, I'm confused. My eyes are open and I'm lying on my back, and for a moment I don't recognize where I am. Slowly my mind frames in the surroundings, and I turn my head to the right. Jane is asleep, a lank of hair fallen over her eyes. I glance around, moving only my head, slowly, quietly, not wanting to wake her. There's light coming in from the window, but *it seems like it's getting dark out* I'm not sure what time it is or how long we've been asleep. I'm not sure how long we were in bed before we were asleep. *Must've been at least an hour.* I feel the need to urinate; it's sudden and strong, and I ease myself out of bed on the side opposite Jane, who doesn't move.

I exit the bedroom; fortunately, the bathroom is the next door over. I urinate and rinse my hands. I glance at my watch; it's 14:57. *We must've fucked longer than I realized. Or slept longer.* I pad softly back into the bedroom, or try to. The latch clicks loudly when I shut the door, and Jane stirs. I tiptoe over next to the bed and she sits up a little bit, the sheet mostly covering her. "Nice." Her voice has a sleepy heaviness to it. I realize she's looking at my crotch and glance down, almost automatically, at the thought. Jane yawns. "Well, it's not like I could forget how big you are, but I kinda forgot what it looks like when you're just walking around." She yawns again. "Not like I've seen you walking around naked lately."

I sit on the opposite side of the bed and scoot over, slide under the blanket with her. She immediately snuggles her head against me and is making a soft mewing sound. *God, it's easy to forget how everything ended.* Jane mumbles something, but her face is buried against me and I can't make it out.

"What's that?"

She tilts her head so her mouth is facing away from my skin and repeats herself, with a tone as though it's taking an enormous effort. "What time is it, anyway?"

"Oh. It's just about 15." I check my watch. It reads 15:00 exactly. "It's exactly fifteen, actually."

Jane yawns into my side. "Fifteen?" She's silent for a moment, and then says, expressionlessly, "Oh." She drags her face away from my flesh and languorously leans back, head lolling slightly to one side, as though she's too sleepy to sit upright. "I forgot. You with your military time."

I blink at her. "Twenty-four—"

"Twenty-four hour time. Excuse me. I forgot." Jane yawns again and snuggles her face back up against my shoulder. She mumbles something.

I pause for a moment. "What—what's that?" softly.

Jane lifts her mouth away from my shoulder slightly. "I was thinking. Counting. Minus twelve. So it's three o'clock in inefficient human person time."

I smile and kiss the top of her head. "Yeah. Three p.m. for you."

Jane pulls herself up a bit and grabs my face, kisses me forcefully. She bites my bottom lip a bit as she pulls away. She's looking intently in my eyes. "What is the absolute latest you have to be home?"

I swallow hard and open my mouth a bit. I can feel myself starting to get hard again, just a tingle, but distinct; I can feel the blood. "Well. I mean I probably need to charge the car for another—for another couple hours anyway. Just to be on the safe side."

Jane puts her hand on my chest, runs it slowly downward. "Better stay plugged in then..."

***

The next time I look at my watch, it's past 16. The light coming through the window is actually brighter; I realized at some point while we were doing it that it was raining outside, that that was why the light had been so dim before. It came to me suddenly; I paused for a moment, and all of a sudden heard teeming rain on the window pane. We shifted positions and I glanced over and could see the rain was coming down so hard that drops were bouncing off the window pane, making little arcs back up towards the sky, like miniature water fountain streams slowed down to individual bursts of water. All this shot through my head, the realization why it had seemed dark, the ferocity of the rain, in the instant between pausing and switching positions on the bed. For the rest of the hour, I didn't think about the rain.

I just now pulled my jeans on, and I take my cell phone out of my pants. Jane is wrapped up in the blanket, still nude underneath. I glance at the screen of the phone and chuckle. Jane shifts under her blanket. "What is it?" Her voice is far away-sounding, dreamy.

"It's Amy." I glance at Jane.

"Oh, Amy." She adjusts the blanket over her shoulder and sneaks her arm out to touch my side, by my ribs. I shiver and flinch.

"That tickles!"

"Sorry." She lays her hand on the top of my thigh. "What'd Amy have to say that was funny?"

"Oh." I smile slightly at Jane, then look back at my phone, at the message. "She texted me. Earlier, apparently; I didn't notice it until just now, but she must've sent it—well, it looks like she must've sent it right after we left the diner. Well, after we started driving, I mean."

"O.K..."

"She said—" I chuckle again softly. "She said, 'Good luck with Jane today.' " I look over at Jane, expectantly.

There's a pause, then Jane snorts and starts giggling. I laugh too. She's nodding. "Well," she says after a moment, "I guess it worked." Jane lies back flat on the pillow and scrunches under the blanket. "Somebody got lucky, anyway."

I smile. "Yeah. Yeah, seriously."

Jane closes her eyes. "No, but seriously, Jack. That was good." She opens her eyes and looks at me. "Really. Both times."

I smile. "Both times, eh?"

She raises an eyebrow. "Well, all five times, if you want to look at it that way." She eyeballs me.

"Oh, really?"

Jane slams her head back against the pillow. "Mmmm hmmm." She sighs. "Well, that part of our relationship was never a problem, anyway."

"Yeah, you can say that again."

"Yeah."

I'm silent for a moment, looking at her. Her eyes are closed, her head resting on the pillow. The rain has ceased, and it's brighter outside than it was earlier. *It'll be dark soon though. I'd better get going or I'll have to drive home in the dark.* I pause. "Jane..."

"Mmmm." Jane's eyes are still closed. She seems like she might be about to fall back asleep.

"Listen."

"Hmmm?"

I lean over so my mouth is close to her head. "I have to go," I whisper. She makes a little sound, a whimper. "Shhh." I shush her and smooth her hair over her forehead. "I don't like to drive when it's dark out when I don't know where I'm going."

Jane sighs. "I know." Her voice is quiet. *Sad?*

I kiss her forehead. "Listen."

"Mmm?"

"Do you—I mean, we could..." my voice, whispering, trails off.

Jane opens her eyes. "Yeah."

I close my eyes and sigh. "Yeah." *Yeah, we're going to get together again. Soon.*

Jane feels for my hand and squeezes it. "Jack?"

I open my eyes. *She's crying!* Jane's eyes are shining, and as I watch, a tear streaks down out of the corner of her eye, down into the pillow. "Honey...what is it?"

Jane closes her eyes and is silent. Her throat moves, and I see another tear streak down the side of her face. She squeezes my hand harder. She takes a shuddering breath and opens her eyes. She's squeezing my hand and looking at me. "Do you—do you have to go?" She bites her lip. "Would you—" She shakes her head. "Oh, God!" she says this loud and violently slams her head back against the pillow. "Ugh, I'm being ridiculous." She sits up and grasps my hand with both her hands, tight. Her hands are wet; she must've wiped her tears and I didn't notice. She looks at me, her eyes a little bloodshot now. "Jack, will you stay here tonight. I know it's stupid and I'm being emotional, but I just—I just want to —"

"Shhh, shhh..." I withdraw my hand and wrap my arms around her. Jane sobs quietly against my shoulder. "It's O.K. I can stay."

Jane cries quietly for another minute and then slows down, sniffles a bit and pulls her head up slightly, then settles it back down in the crook of my neck. I'm only wearing jeans; I hadn't put my shirt on yet, and Jane traces my collarbone with her finger. "I mean, we have plenty more to talk about anyway, right?" She glances up at me, which I see out of the corner of my eye.

I pet the side of her head, her hair. "Yeah. Yeah, we definitely have plenty to talk about."

Jesus. What am I going to tell Amy?

Chapter 11

We're in the kitchen, and Jane is making some kind of soup. She's been explaining to me how she's become a vegetarian—a vegan, actually, no cheese or eggs or anything—and she's been researching all this stuff on how to beat cancer naturally. *She's changed a lot, that's for sure.* I'm sitting at the little table in the kitchen, only a few feet from the stove, watching her back. She turns and looks at me. "Am I talking too much?"

"No! No, definitely not." I lean forward a bit. "I'm listening. I'm just—I guess I'm just taking it all in." Jane and I look at each other for a moment, her standing by the stove, holding a wooden spoon *"important to only use wooden utensils..."* and me sitting at the table, fidgeting with my cell phone, fingering it idly where it sits.

Jane glances at my fingers idly knocking the corner of my cell phone back and forth, rotating the device a scant amount in opposite directions with each tap. "Got a call to make, Mr. Popular?" She smirks and turns back to her stew or whatever it is.

I clear my throat. "Actually, you reminded me." I hunch forward and grasp the phone and unlock it. "I should probably text Amy, let her know I won't be home tonight."

Jane is silent as I'm tapping softly on the screen. I've only typed, "Hey Aim..." *I am not sure how to say this.* I realize Jane just said something. "Sorry, I didn't catch that. Could you say it again?"

I glance up and Jane is stirring the pot with measured motions, slowly, purposefully. A moment passes while I watch her. "I said," she says finally, "what are you going to tell Amy?" I don't respond and after a moment, Jane rests the wooden spoon against the side of the pot and turns her head towards me, her eyebrows arched. The question is hanging silently in the air.

I blink several times. I shake my head. "I don't know. I was just—I was just thinking about that." I glance down at my phone. "Hey Aim..." stares back at me, mockingly. I smile. "So far, I wrote, 'Hey Aim.' What do you think?"

"Good start!" Jane is nodding and turns back to her stew. She has some vegetables cut and begins adding them in a particular order according to her own internal calculus. After a few soft plops, she speaks again. "Why not just tell her that things went well and you're staying overnight with me?"

Again the question hangs silently in the air, not the question she asked, but the question she didn't ask: *does Amy have a problem with me?* and, maybe more importantly: *how much does she know about what happened?*

I close my eyes and let the room settle away into the darkness. At this point I'm fairly practiced at clearing my mind, but it seems like it's been a long time since I've had a clear mind, since before I got the letter from Jane. *God was that only this past Friday? Here I am in Perkasie, sitting at her table, watching her make soup. After...* I let my thoughts coalesce and drift into a container in my mind. I let the container drift away, and my mind is clear. I hear myself speaking. "We don't have to talk about this right now, but no. I never told Amy anything about what happened." I pause; my eyes are still closed, and I imagine Jane standing frozen, silently, at the stove. I continue, slowly. "And that means... that is, I think that means." I stop. I recoalesce the invading thoughts, appearing like red fire flickering across my mind. I take a deep breath. My eyes are still closed, and I don't know if Jane is watching me or not. "I don't think. I know. I know Amy..." I pause and take another breath. *If this is hard to say, then there is something there. I have work to do. I have been carrying this, burying this, for a long time.* "Amy doesn't know anything about what happened with Jenny." *Not why what happened happened, and not the other thing that happened.* "And so... I'm sorry, Jane." I open my eyes.

Jane turns around and looks at me. She doesn't say anything, she's just standing there holding a wooden spoon, steam rolling out of the giant pot next to her. From my perspective the steam is right in front of her, but further back, and it seems to be almost too dramatic, like a low-budget fog machine effect, highlighting her standing there, with the spoon.

"I'm sorry. I never talked to her about what happened—what happened with us. With you and me splitting up. I just told her that we were having problems, and she assumed that it had to do with Jenny... I mean of course she did, and..." I stop. Jane hasn't moved; the rolling steam, the wooden spoon clutched in her right hand, her left hand on her hip, turned towards me, watching me expressionlessly. I close my eyes and take a deep breath and once again collect everything in between me and my next statement into an energetic container and whisk it away to another place in my mind. I open my eyes. "I know she blames you. And I let her." *There, I said it.* I stare at Jane, expectantly.

Jane doesn't move. She's just looking at me. After a moment, she speaks, startling me. "And?"

"And what?"

Jane squints at me slightly. "That was what you just spent five minutes trying to spit out. Amy blames me for us splitting up, or for Jenny killing herself, or for whatever—" here she turns back to her stew. "—for all of it. *That* is what you've been trying to spit out?" Her voice isn't angry. "Well," she turns back towards me, still stirring, just turning her head and torso. "No shit, Sherlock. I blame me, too. Blamed. Blame. I don't know." She sighs and turns back to stirring. "I mean—I blamed myself for years. I think that's how I grew myself some cancer. So now, I'm like fuck all that. I don't care if it is my fault." She glances back at me, quickly. "Not that I 'don't care', you know."

"No, I know what you're saying."

Jane looks at me for another moment, then busies herself with partitioning vegetables and plopping them in. "I guess that's the problem," she says after a small silence. "I mean, I care about all of it. I care about you, you know."

I'm watching her. "I know you do, hon." *Maybe I should do something.* I stand up and walk next to her, lean awkwardly against the counter next to the stove, far enough away to not be in the way of her vegetables, but otherwise as near as I can. We're now next to each other, two feet away, me with my back to the counter, my head and torso turned sideways and my hips facing where I'd just been sitting, she to my left, facing the stove, her face intent, the steam roiling up around her face. "I know you care. I knew you did then, too."

Jane glances up at me then quickly back down. She's focusing on the stew *completely out of proportion to anything that's actually happening in that pot* and her voice is slow and measured. "That's why I wanted to talk to you, Jack." She stirs slowly, deliberately, meditatively. "There is —there is a lot that is between us that hasn't been said." She looks over at me, her hand frozen now, holding the *wooden* spoon. "Holding all this—all that garbage inside me was literally poisoning me. I had to let it go. I *have* to let it go. I need to let it out and let myself heal."

I'm nodding. I pause for a moment *in case she wants to say more* and then, gently, "Jane..."

She'd been looking back down into the stew, and now she looks over at me quickly. She doesn't say anything, and I continue, my voice soft *I don't want to trigger her about anything* "I may be able to help."

Jane chuckles and goes back to her stew with a vengeance. "You are winning the 'No shit, Sherlock' award for sure, tonight. That's twice now." She shoves some more vegetables into the stew and then turns to fully face me. "I know you like doing everything twice."

I smile. *She's referring to this afternoon.* "No, no, not doing everything." I'm smiling at her, and she's smiling back, but her smile fades slightly. "I *buy* two of everything. I don't necessarily *do* things twice. Unless," I reach out and poke her under the ribs, teasingly, "it's worth it."

She half smiles at me, literally smiles with one side of her mouth. "Well, yeah. You always said that orgasms are healthy."

"They are!"

"I know, I know. I know more than you know..." She winks at me. "But seriously, I thought you were supposed to be some kind of genius. No shit you can help me. That's why I wrote you that letter."

I'm staring at her, and she's staring at me. After a moment, I say, "It was a lovely letter."

"*Thank* you," she tips her head at me as she says this.

"You know—sealing the letter itself—with the sealing wax—from our wedding..."

Jane looks up at me quickly. "I was hoping —"

I put my hand on her shoulder. "It was lovely." There are tears in my eyes now, and I blink. "Really. It was sweet."

Jane sighs. "I did it almost without thinking about it, like automatically, and then afterwards I wondered if it was a mistake."

"No. No, not at all. It was lovely. It was—" I pause to think of the right word. "Touching."

Jane nods, watching me. She takes another sigh. "Good." She turns back to her pot and stirs. She cocks her head sideways at me and says, with the half-smile back, "I wanted to touch you..."

I smile. I close my eyes and shake my head, and open them and smile. *She looks so happy right now.* "I guess I did, too. Want you to touch me. In more ways than one, obviously."

#

Jane and I are sitting at the little table. The giant pot of stew or soup or whatever it is is sitting between us, still half full despite my having had two large bowls of it myself.

Ratatouille. I think Jane said this is called ratatouille. I always thought ratatouille was some kind of pasta, but I guess it's some kind of stew. Or soup. Or stew. I glance up from the last spoonful of my second bowl and see that Jane is watching me. "What?" I swipe the spoon in and out of my mouth fluidly, withdrawing the last spoonful of the vegan ratatouille. "This is fantastic, by the way. Did I tell you that already?"

"About three times, but that's O.K., I like hearing it." Jane is still watching me. She leans forward and peaks into the huge pot in the center of the table, sitting on a wooden pedestal instead of a cloth mat. *I hadn't noticed that before. I don't think it's related to the woodenness of the spoon, but I don't know. I'll have to ask her some time. Maybe they were a set or something.* Peering into the pot, Jane says, "There's plenty more if you want another bowl...? Or even a half a bowl..." She glances up at me, still leaning over to peer into the huge pot.

I pause. "I think I'm good." Jane leans back, then pauses halfway and cocks her head slightly at me.

"You sure...?" I hesitate, and Jane smiles a little bit, and moves for the wooden spoon.

110

"I know what that means. Hand me your bowl."

I can feel myself smiling. "Just a half—oh what the heck." I watch Jane fill my bowl. "I don't know if I'm going to regret this, but right now I'm not. It's *delicious*."

Jane finishes spooning the ratatouille into my bowl and hands it to me. "Thank you."

"No, really. Thank *you*. This is a real treat." I pause. "I always did like your cooking."

Jane cocks her head at me, raising an eyebrow. "Oh, you liked my cooking, did you?"

I smile. "*Loved* it, O.K.? I *loved* your cooking. Love, actually. I *love* your cooking, present tense." I stir the stew—the ratatouille—and take a spoonful. It's still steaming, and I blow softly on it.

"Actually, I was thinking something earlier, but I got distracted when you told me for the fourth or fifth time how great the stew came out."

"Stew? I thought you said it's ratatouille?"

Jane squints at me. "It *is* ratatouille. Ratatouille is a kind of stew, more or less." Jane half smiles. "Jeez, Mr. Precision."

I give a shrug with my eyebrows and swallow the presumably now-cooled spoonful of ratatouille or stew. "You know me."

"I know, I know. Mathematics is all about precision." Jane closes her eyes for a moment. *Looking thoughtful. Like remembering.* "But what I was going to say —what I was going to say before was, did you ever text your sister back?" I look up at Jane, startled. "Amy...?"

"Oh shit." I set the spoon down with its bowl resting in the ratatouille. I reach for my pocket to retrieve my cell phone, but it's not there. "Shit. My phone."

"Oh I put it on the counter. Over there..." she gestures to the far counter, away from the stove and things, where there are a few non-cooking-related items. I get up to retrieve my phone. "You'd left it on the table, and I wanted to set it for dinner."

I'm standing at the counter, having just picked up my phone, my back to Jane. *She set the table for dinner.* I turn around swiftly. *This is kind of like a date.* I look at Jane. She's looking at me expectantly. "Are you going to text her? I mean—" she glances down at her empty bowl, seems to consider for a moment, then lifts it over to the pot and serves herself another half bowl. "Did you figure out what to say?"

I'm looking at Jane, at the table with the pot of fancy stew *she said it's peasant stew actually* on its fancy wooden pot holder. *She set the table. I wonder if she thinks of this—if she intends for this to be a date...* "I don't know." I pause. "I guess I could say that I'm having a date with my ex wife." Jane looks at me, her face expressionless. "Excuse me." I close my eyes briefly and shake my head. "*Former* wife. I made a commitment to not refer to you as my 'ex' wife. I'm sorry."

Jane is looking at me, her eyes squinting slightly. "O.K." She's still looking at me. "Well..." She makes a sort of "ahem" sound, daintily, not really clearing her throat. She leans over and sips some of the stew gingerly, her eyes rolled up to look at me. She pauses halfway through that one spoonful *that must be why she eats so much slower than I do* and cocks her head at me again. "You *could* say that, I suppose." She

113

finishes her spoonful and sits back up in her chair. "If that's what you'd call this."

I look at her. She's leaning back in her chair, watching me. The unasked question hangs in the air. "I'm sorry, I—" I shake my head and walk back to sit across from her at the table. "I was just trying to be funny, I guess. Not funny, but... I don't know." I've been studiously looking down at the phone in my hands while saying this, and now I glance up at Jane.

Jane reaches a hand across the table, and I take her hand. She's leaning forward a bit, and so am I, and we're holding hands. She reaches out with her other hand and holds my hand with both of hers, looking at me. "Jack..." Her eyes are wide open now.

"Yeah."

"It's O.K., I'm sorry. I know this is all very confusing, it's confusing for me. I wasn't trying to—I mean I didn't plan any of this, you know."

I set my phone down on the table and reach out with my other hand also, so we're both holding both of each others' hands. We're sort of scooted to one side of the big pot, and Jane unceremoniously shoves the pot—

fancy wooden potholder, fancy stew, and all —off to the side of the table, so we can hold hands uninterruptedly. Jane is looking at me with those big eyes. *I don't know what to say.* "I don't know what to say." A flash goes across her face, and I add quickly, "I mean, I don't mean that badly." I lean over and pull her hands up to my face and kiss her knuckles, first on one hand, then the other. She withdraws her right hand *she's right-handed* and, with me still holding it, places it on the side of my face. We look into each others' eyes for a few moments, then gradually withdraw.

We settle back into our seats, and Jane is the first to speak. "Eat your ratatouille before it gets cold." She proceeds to eat hers, and I follow suit. The handle of my spoon is hot from the spoon sitting in the stew. *It probably acts as a radiator, though; the soup is probably cooler now. Ratatouille —the ratatouille is probably cooler now than it would have been, because of the spoon sitting in it, absorbing and radiating its heat.*

We eat together in silence for a few minutes. I'm mostly looking at my food, but I cast furtive glances up at Jane, and we catch eyes at one point. *She was probably*

115

doing the same thing. Eventually, I notice my phone sitting on the side of the table. "Shit. I still need to figure out what to say."

Jane puts down her spoon. "Well... Do you have to tell her that you won't be home? I mean don't you guys live your own lives?"

"Well, yeah, I mean of course. We pretty much each do our own thing. I mean we hang out and stuff, but... I don't know. I think that if I weren't coming home..." I stop talking. *Think. What would happen if I just don't come home and don't say anything about it. Probably nothing. Maybe?* "I guess I just feel like, out of respect or something. I don't know. She's my sister, and I..." I stop. *I'm over-thinking this.* "You know, I think I'm over-thinking this. If we were just roommates, or housemates—if we were just housemates, two people who lived in the same house but weren't otherwise related or involved—I don't think that I would tell her whether I was coming home—I mean not coming home—I don't think I would tell her that I was not coming home any particular night." Jane's nodding. I nod. "Yeah, I think I should just text her something simple." I unlock the phone and my partially composed message is on the screen. "Hey

Aim..." I add to it, "busy day, sry. Thanks for wishing me luck, it went better than I thought it would. Love you" I set down the phone and look up.

Jane is looking at me wide-eyed. After a moment, she says, the words bursting out, "So...? What did you finally say?"

I chuckle and spoon myself some ratatouille. "I just said, 'hey Aim, sorry for not writing back, busy day. today went better than I thought."

Jane giggles. She nods. "Yeah. I mean—" She shakes her head. "Well, put." I smile at her. "It really is going better than I thought too, and you know, I really had no idea—I mean, I wasn't like planning to invite you back here or anything."

"No?"

"No." She's looking at me. *I'm not sure what she's thinking.*

"What changed your mind? Or, I mean—gave you the idea. What made you think to?"

Jane stares at me for a moment. "Honestly?"

117

I snort softly. "Well, yeah."

Jane closes her eyes for a moment. "Honestly... O.K., don't judge me... When you got up to go—when we saw the Philly parking meter cop coming towards your car, and you got up to go. I was still sitting on the stairs. Remember?"

I think back. "Yeah. I mean, sure, I remember. It was just this morning, silly."

Jane smiles. "Well, when you stood up and turned to face me, I was eye-level with your crotch." The corners of her mouth are twitching. I smile, and she smiles more and shakes her head. "What can I say? I saw the bulge and I—felt the pulse."

I smile and nod. "It's O.K., I understand completely."

"Phew!"

"No, I mean it. When we were walking out of the diner..."

Jane gets an "ah ha" look on her face. "I was walking out first. Huh." She levels her gaze at me. "You were checking out my ass, weren't you?"

I smile and look down briefly, then back up at her. "What can I say? Booty like that make a grown man cry." We both laugh, and I finish my ratatouille.

***

It's an hour later, and we're sitting on the couch, and it comes up out of nowhere. We aren't talking about anything in particular, and then Jane says, "Oh, I keep meaning to ask you—I can't believe I didn't ask you this all day. I didn't mean to be rude, I kept thinking it and then we'd be talking about something else and I'd get distracted and forget, and then later something would make me remember, and we'd be—" she stops and glances down briefly, smilingly, "—busy, or something." She gives me a quick pointed stare. I smile. "But anyway, I never asked you. What do you do these days? You're not teaching are you?"

I look at her steadily. *It's now or never. If I tell her, if I explain it, she's going to want to do it. If she does it, it's gonna come out. Karl will know.* "Actually, I still teach part-time. Online. Here and there, it's like real part-time. A few different schools around the country, every few months I'll teach for a few months. A couple of them are steady, a couple are intermittent. It's easy work for the money." She's looking at me. "It's not much money, really, but the work is easy and the students—well, they vary, but I focus on the ones that are grateful, and so it's gratifying."

Jane is still looking at me. I'm looking back. She squints a bit. "You—I don't think you really answered my question."

I could do the process with her, instead of Karl, maybe. I smile. "Well, there's more to the answer, for sure, but I have a question too." *But Karl would have to help me with the analysis anyway. It wouldn't work.* I'm stalling. "What made you think that I wasn't teaching anymore?"

Jane squints again, accusingly, but not meanly. "You're not off the hook for my question, yet, but I'll answer yours, since it's easy enough." Jane leans over and picks up her can of unsweetened seltzer water *ever dramatic* and takes a sip, holding the can close to her mouth when she's finished, like she's about to take another sip. "I googled you." She points at me with the can in a short swift motion. "Now your turn," and she takes another sip.

I'm watching her lips, watching her lick her lips after she lowers the can and before she places it back on the little table by the couch *on a coaster.* "You googled me?"

"Oh my God, quit stalling. What do you *do* now?" Her voice is whiny, but not in earnest. "Yeah, of course I googled you. Your old school didn't come up, so I figured you weren't there any more."

I'm looking at her. "Anything—anything that did come up?"

"Well, I found out your address, didn't I?" Jane kicks me, lightly, from across the couch. "Now c'mon, gimme a break. What're you a spy now, huh?" Jane suddenly sits bolt upright. "You didn't—you didn't end up getting a job with the NSA did you? Is that why you can't say?"

"Oh God no!" *I rarely blaspheme.* I shake my head. "No, even if I wanted to—I, ah— wouldn't want to go through their—ah, intake procedure."

Jane looks at me. "Why not?"

I take a short breath. "I knew a guy who joined and he described it to me." I take a sip of my own seltzer. It tastes exactly like bubbles, only somehow it seems slightly spicy. "Let's just say that you have to tell them every detail about your life." I look at her steadily. "Every detail." I pause. "And they're particularly interested in the—um, let's say juicy details." Jane's looking at me. *We are both thinking about the same thing, or at least about one of the two same things, right now.* "Oh, and you're connected to a lie detector, and talking to people who are the world experts in figuring out stuff, especially cryptic stuff. So you have to tell them *everything.*"

Jane nods slowly. "I see." She thinks for a moment, and begins slowly. "Jack..."

"Mhm."

She's looking down at her hands. "Jack, have you ever... Have you told anyone, I mean anyone?"

She's looking at her hands, but I'm looking at her eyes. "No." She looks up, and our eyes meet. "No."

"Not even a therapist?"

"Fuck no." I must've said it louder than I meant, because she flinches a bit. "I'm

122

sorry. It's just—no, I mean I haven't told *any*one."

Jane is quiet again. She's looking at her hands again. "I did. Tell a therapist, I mean." She looks up at me. I nod. "I think it helped. He said I ought to talk to you about it, that we really ought to talk about it." She spreads her hands. "I mean, that's how *this* all got started."

"Yeah, I mean that makes sense." *This has literally been killing her. I've got to tell her.* "Jane..."

She's looking at me. "Jack...?"

"I, uh, didn't answer your question before. Not really."

"I know." She smiles.

I take a deep breath. "I run a company. I mean, I'm co-owner. Karl and I run it together."

"Karl! Oh he—"

I hold up my hand. "Let me get this out. I've been meaning to tell you all day" *that's only partly true* "—I mean, I've been thinking about telling you as much as you've been thinking about asking me." I take a deep

123

breath. "Our company—what we do—we specialize in helping people..."

Jane nods. "O.K...?"

Now I'm the one glancing at my hands, and I force myself to look up and into her eyes. "What we do is, specifically—we help people, using a kind of meditation process. We have a specialized process..." I glance down at my hands again. *Just say it. Saying it isn't going to do anything.* "Jane, it's like this. What we do is mostly, we mostly work with veterans and—people with PTSD." I let that hang in the air for a second. *People like you and me.* I take a breath and realize only as I'm saying it that my voice is shaky and quiet: "People like you and me. Also. People who have been through something that's—that's really affected them, and they're trying to get—to be free of any problems."

Jane's eyes are wide. Her mouth is open but she's not speaking. I close my eyes and wait a moment *put everything else in the energy container. Just be here now.* I open my eyes and Jane's mouth is still open, but she closes it and says, "Jack. Oh my God." I nod. "Oh my God. Can I do that—process?—with you? That's exactly what I need! Does it work? You've done it, right?"

"Yes." *Yes it works, no I haven't done it.* "It works really really well, actually. That's why, uh—why it didn't come up when you googled me. We get almost all of our business from the government, from veterans, and we get a lot of high-end clients. It's all very hush-hush." I'm looking at her. "Big wigs don't want the world to know they hired the ultimate shrink, or whatever."

Jane closes her eyes. "Thank you, God." *Amen.* She opens her eyes and looks at me. "When can I do it? How do I sign up?"

It's about to get complicated. "I'll have to—I mean, I'm sure we can figure something out. It pays to know someone, right?"

For an answer, Jane flings her arms around me—springs from her end of the couch and nearly tackles me on my end and flings her arms around me, is more accurate. By the time I put my arms around her, I can feel her sobbing against me. "It's gonna be O.K." *I hope.*

Chapter 12

We're lying in bed together later that night. I've been lying awake for a long time. *It's got to be after midnight by now*. I don't want to look at my watch. *Probably well after midnight.* I know how to put myself to sleep in a very short period of time, minutes at the very most, but for some reason, I don't. *Not just now. I never use our methods to put myself to sleep.* I like to lie awake at night and think. I spend so much time during the day controlling thoughts, my thoughts, and other people's thoughts, I think that there is something alluring about just letting my mind wander. I let myself think about anything *not anything—not that* that comes to it, follow tangential thoughts, wonder about stuff that doesn't matter. Sometimes I engage in fantasies about different imaginary situations; sometimes I just think about things I need to do the next day. I wait until sleep naturally overtakes my mind. It's the one time I'm letting my brain control my thoughts "in the wild".

Right now I'm thinking about Jane, lying asleep next to me. *She would always conk out almost as soon as her head hit the pillow.* I glance over and try to make out her features in the dim light coming through the window. *Must be a streetlight nearby.* A lock of her hair has fallen across her face, and I want to brush it behind her ear but I'm afraid of waking her. I gently, slowly, reach my hand out, brushing my fingers lightly across her forehead as I move the hair. She shifts slightly and makes a murmuring sound, then scootches her whole body closer to me. *She must be only lightly asleep. When she's deep asleep, nothing could wake her.* I watch her face for another moment and then turn back on my back.

Earlier, on the couch, Jane sobbed against my shoulder for a while. Eventually she got up and brought our empty seltzer cans to the recycling; she brought us fresh cans, and it was almost by mutual unvoiced agreement that we didn't broach the subject again. I'd already decided by that point that I would talk to Karl about it the next day—tomorrow—and I figured Jane figured I'd get back to her about it, obviously as soon as possible. We both seemed to realize that there wasn't anything more to be said about the subject. If we said anything more about the subject, it might lead us to *the* subject—the one she needed a therapist to talk to anyone about, and that I hadn't spoken about to anyone at all, therapist or otherwise. *And I'm not going to think about it now.*

I'm lying on my back and I close my eyes, and I see Jenny. She's standing in the sun. We're at the beach, and I'd just looked up at her. She'd called my name, and I looked up. *She was wearing a two-piece bikini. It was blue.* Jenny laughed; I'd been staring at my feet. I looked at her, and she walked towards me through the inch-deep water of the wave coming in.

"What were you just thinking about?" Jenny's eyes seemed to always sparkle when she talked. Except when she was mad; when she was mad, her eyes looked murky. Sometimes she'd be mad and she'd be hiding it, but I could always tell, because her eyes looked murky to me. They were still brilliantly, startlingly green, but there was something different about them when she was upset. Not right then, though— standing in the sun after calling my name, and then walking through the inch-deep incoming wave water, her eyes were just sparkling—even more brilliant than usual, because of the bright sun.

"What?"

Jenny is right next to me now, in front of me, standing a foot away. I can see the mole under her left armpit, just outside the fabric of her bikini top, as she fiddles with her hair. "I said," she releases a great wave of hair—she must've been pulling off her ponytail holder—"what were you thinking about?" We are both twenty-three years old.

"Oh." I look down at my feet. The wave has crested and the water is now receding, and the undertow is pulling sand out from underneath my feet, burying them little by slowly. A depression has formed around my feet as the incoming wave washes sand to try to fill in the hole, and the outgoing wave tries to wash it away. The sand is swirling around my feet as the outgoing wave water rushes past. I can feel a little more sand erode from under my feet. "I was watching the sand."

There are noises of a beach at the New Jersey shore: kids screaming, a far-off sound of a nearby airplane trailing an advertisement, and the steady, ever-present, background roar of the waves. There's no sound from Jenny, and I look up. She bursts out laughing. Still laughing, she is nearly incomprehensible, but I can understand her no matter how she talks, and can clearly make out: "the sand?" Her laughter slows a bit, and, composed, she repeats, "The sand? I thought you were supposed to be some kind of genius. The *sand?*" She pauses, the laughter gone. "What about the sand were you watching, specifically?"

I look steadily at her, at her green eyes. She's only about a foot away, and I can see the little yellow star surrounding each pupil. "I was watching the swirls of sand when the tide's going out. Around my feet."

Jenny doesn't seem to change her expression; anyone but me wouldn't be able to tell that her expression had changed, anyway, but I can see it: her eyes are sparkling in a different way than usual. She's amused. *She's not going to settle for that.* "...and...?"

"And." I glance down at the sand. The next wave has come and is now going, and the sand is swirling. I see my feet, and, above them in my view, Jenny's. *We have the save toes.* I look up at Jenny's sparkling, amused, eyes. "And, I was thinking about how the swirls of sand in the little pool here are governed by differential equations, how they swirl I mean, and I was wondering how deep the pool has to be and how fast the water has to recede for the swirls to be orderly, and likewise for them to be chaotic. I was wondering whether the onset of the chaotic regime is related predominantly to moon phase—which I suspect is a factor one way or the other—or is more dependent on more local factors like temperature, or even wind speed—though wind speed, of course, is itself determined by differential equations, and could be considered somewhat epiphenomenal to the actual underlying variables."

Jenny's mouth opens slowly in a smile, and then suddenly she bursts forward at me, wrapping her arms around me and laughing and grabbing my hands and dancing in a circle around me. I smile and laugh and spin in a circle, and she is shouting, "Wheeee!" and "Wooo hooo!" and then she lets go of my left hand with her right and starts dragging me in a wide arc, jumping up and down and squealing, loudly, "My little brother is a genius! My little brother is a genius! What do you think of that dirty Jerz?!" and with a final yank she pulls both of us down into the clean white sand of Cape May. I'm laughing, and she's laughing, and we're lying on our sides, and it's the sunflowers again, only that time I was on my right side, and she on her left, and this time I'm on my left and she on her right, and the sunflowers are sand and beachgoers and the sound of the crashing waves, and we've both flopped on our backs after the laugh wears off, until finally I turn my head to the left, and she turns her head to the right, and we're lying on the sand, still holding hands.

"Jenny?"

"Jack?"

"You know what you are?"

"What, Jackie?"

I try to hold my face still but I can feel myself about to lose control, so I swallow quickly and blurt out, "You're. A." I sit up and lean on my elbow for emphasis, and she props her head on her hand and looks at me expectantly *politely*. I feel my mouth

133

twitching, and by the time I say it, I'm laughing, and she's laughing: "Loon!"

"Oh, *I*'m a loon? *I*'m a loon?" Jenny sits up enough to poke my ribs and tickle me a bit, but I instinctively twitch away—she knows I don't like to be tickled, and it was only a half-hearted attempt—and lays back, her chest heaving to catch her breath after the spinning and the laughing and the hilarity of my comparison. *Her mole is not in view right now.* Lying on the sand, her hair a red halo in the blindingly white sand, she says to me, matter-of-factly, "Jack, really. I think we could take a survey. What do you think?" She jerks her head upwards left and right, still lying on the sand, looking at me. "I think, I *think* that if we asked all these people here on this beach, which of the two of us—" she stifles a chuckle, but I can see it reverberate down her body, like a shock wave, and when it gets to her feet, she gives a little kick, like a release of static electricity, grounding itself out—"which of the two of us, is more of a," she pauses and lifts her head from the sand, "a *loon*—" she purses her lips into a distinct "O" shape and I close my eyes to stifle a laugh. Jenny lays her head back in the sand and her eyes are closed and her voice is dreamy, playful. "I am pretty sure that if we explained how I was playing in the waves... wearing a bikini, you know, making little splashes, you know—*beach* stuff, whereas you—not ten feet away, also in the—" she snorts "technically, *technically*, also in the—in the *surf*—" she giggles and sighs. "Yeah. I think if we explained how I was splashing and having beach fun and you were, well, technically *on* the beach, technically *in* the water—"

"Halfway. Or half-time, really. All the way, half the time."

Jenny sits up on her elbow again and looks at me. "O.K. Jackie, I will grant that you were only, even technically, *in* the water, *half* the time. But I will not say that you were 'all the way' in the water for that half. No. Sir." She lays back down.

Jenny is silent for a moment. "Jenny?"

"Hmm?"

"I think you didn't finish your thought?"

"What's that?" her voice is dreamy again, more dreamy than playful.

"You were in the middle of saying that if we surveyed these people and explained how you were playing in the water and I was standing in the water, and you stopped."

"Hmm. Yeah. That's true."

"I think you were going to make the point that, if you explained that I was contemplating the differential equations that governed whence the sand swirls by my feet were in a chaotic regime—that, I'm presuming that you were going to say that you think that they would agree that I were the loon, in that case."

Jenny shields the sun from her eyes with her hand and opens her right eye, just her right eye, just a slit. *She's sleepy. She makes the same face when she's waking up in the morning and isn't ready to yet. She calls it waking up 'one eye at a time'.* She nods slightly. "Jackie..."

"Yeah."

"They would definitely say that."

I smile and lay down on the sand with my shoulder against hers, and she fishes for my left hand with her right. She presses the side of her head against mine and we fall asleep in the sand.

***

"Jackie?"

"Hmm." I'm still asleep but my dream is fading quickly. I start to become aware of Jenny's hand still holding mine, of the brightness of the afternoon sun in Cape May lighting up the insides of my eyelids red. I don't remember what I was dreaming about, but I remember a nice feeling, and I feel drowsy and pleasant. And hot. It's hot, but I have that hot, drowsy, lazy feeling. *Thank God we put on sunscreen earlier. I wonder how long we've been asleep.* I don't want to open my eyes. The red light coming through my closed eyelids is so much brighter than darkness, and I know that the uninterrupted afternoon sun will be piercing. I enjoy the comfortable protection of my eyelids for another moment.

"Jackie... Wake up...." Jenny's voice is far away and I'm starting to drift back into the dream. I can feel her let go of my hand, but I can still feel where she was holding it: there's a sense, a presence, maybe from the pressure of her hand during the time we were asleep oppressing the flow of blood, maybe an electromagnetic resettling of energy flow, maybe just my imagination, but I can still feel Jenny's phantom hand holding mine. The sun freshly shining on my empty hand lends its own mirage, and I can almost imagine the heat of the sun on my open palm as the heat of her hand still pressed there. I still feel her fingers wrapping around the side of my hand *maybe it's sweat trickling down* and even though I know *palms don't sweat from heat only from emotional response* she's let go of my hand and is probably sitting up now, messing with her hair, in my dreamy, drowsy, sun-dappled state I can still feel her hand there almost as vividly as I did seconds before when it in fact was still holding mine.

"Jackie, do you want to get up and go get something to eat?"

"Mmm." I work my mouth; it's dry. "Sure." I clear my throat. I take a breath. The bright red behind my eyes is dimming. *Maybe a cloud overhead. Probably a good time to open my eyes.* "Did you still want..." I let my voice trail off. Something flitted across my mind, quick, shadowy. The phantom feel of Jenny's hand is fading. I'm starting to wake up. *I'm gonna have to brush the sand out of my hair.*

"That's what I was thinking." I hear movement. I think it's Jenny shaking out some of the sand from her hair, but I can't quite tell from the sound, as though it's coming from the wrong side of me.

"O.K." I swallow, dryly. "I suppose I should get up then."

"You don't have to just yet."

I yawn. "What time is it?"

There's a pause. "It's almost seven."

"Almost seven?" My mind is swaying back and forth between sleepiness and wakefulness like the back and forth of the water. My mind clicks. "Why is it so bright still?"

"Daylight savings time, silly."

"Oh." With each visit back and forth between sleeping and waking, my mind is becoming more alert; the sound of the surf is softer as I focus more on Jenny's voice and the time. "We might have to—maybe we can push back our reservations."

"What?"

"I thought we were planning to eat—well, now, I guess."

"Oh, I didn't think we, um..." Jenny's voice trails off. My mind clicks. "Well, if you want to get up now we can eat now, or we could wait a bit if you want."

"Let's see if we can push it back to nineteen-thirty. Did you still want to get seafood?"

"Seafood?"

"Yeah." I sit up and hunch over with my eyes still closed so I won't be facing the sun when I open them. My eyes seem like they're glued together; I'm loathe to finally open them.

"What are you talking about?"

"You know, loon." I smile and rub my eyes. "That place. I don't know what it's called. You made reservations." I pause and turn to look at Jenny. I turned around in my sleep and she's on my right instead of my left.

"Jack—what are you talking about. I told you, I'm a vegan."

I snort. I blink at Jenny, and she's gone, and the surf is silent, and I'm blinking at Jane.

Chapter 13

Jane makes me breakfast. It's delicious, which is no surprise *she was always into cooking* although I am a bit surprised that vegan breakfast can be so good. She serves something remarkably like scrambled eggs but which she assures me *at great length and with details I didn't remember even while she was explaining them* is completely plant-based. When we're finished eating, sitting at the little table with empty plates—multiple empty plates for each of us, because she served a fruit compote with some kind of half-scone, half-pancake affair, along with the scrambled non-eggs—I lean back and gaze across the tableaux of dishes at Jane. "Jane..." I shake my head slowly. "That was delicious." I pick a crumb from the scone-pancake plate and greedily pop it in my mouth. "Mmm." I look at her. "Delicious. I don't know what else to say. I wasn't expecting any of this."

"Even though you had reservations?" She is smirking at me.

I smile and look down for a moment. Looking up, "I was wondering when you were going to bring that up..."

"I'm just teasing you..."

"No, no, I know. I know." I smile. "I was having some kind of a dream. Something about being at a beach..." *Being at the beach at Cape May with Jenny during the summer a few months after we'd both turned twenty-three. We'd had reservations for a seafood place she wanted to try, at nineteen hundred. We fell asleep on the beach and woke up later than we'd planned, and by the time we washed all the sand out of our hair—her hair mostly—and gotten changed and ready for dinner, we knew we would never make the reservations, so we'd called in in advance and pushed them back a half an hour. I can still picture her across the table from me. There was a white linen tablecloth. I had crab cakes. She had salmon, and then she wished she had gotten the crab cakes, and so I gave her one of mine, and she gave me her entire salmon steak. The salmon was served with sauteed mushrooms, shiitake and something I'd never heard of. She taught me that I was supposed to squeeze lemon juice on fish, which for some reason I had never heard of, probably because I rarely ate fish.*

"Do you remember anything else about it?"

I look at Jane across the dishes. I shake my head slightly. "Something about wanting to have seafood I guess."

Jane looks at me. "Well, like I said," she stands up and starts collecting plates, and I hurriedly stack mine and stand up, but she reaches to take them from me and carries the lot of them to the sink, "I'm a vegan. No seafood for you this morning." She gives me the corner of her eye when she turns to the sink.

I follow her and lean my side against the little counter while she washes the dishes. "Here," she hands me a dishtowel, "make yourself useful." I scrunch my face at her and dry the dishes as she hands them to me.

"Jane."

She glances over, dish in hand. There's a blob of partially dried fruit compote and its associated juice stuck to the surface of the plate, its dark purple *blueberry and raspberry, did she remember that I love them or just happen to have them around?* standing out against the white ceramic. She rinses the plate under the faucet, dislodging part but not all of the purplish blob, and she begins to scrub it with a green plastic scrubby pad *I'm almost surprised she's not using some kind of bamboo scrubber or something. I won't say anything* evidently thinking that her glance was sufficient response. I continue. "I was hoping that I *could* be helpful, really helpful, if you're still interested." Jane looks over at me quickly then just as quickly returns her focus to removing the vestiges of the fruit compote blob. "I mean—look, we don't have to talk about it right now, but—I'll talk to Karl today. I don't have anything to do with the scheduling—actually, I'm not sure that he does either, but he at least would know who to talk to, one of the secretaries or something. I guess we have people for that." I'm standing, helplessly waiting for a wet dish. *Stammering.* Jane has stopped scrubbing, is standing there with the faucet running, holding the green scrubby in one hand and the seemingly clean plate in the other. Her eyes are closed. I take a step closer and gingerly lower the handle on the faucet, turning off the water. She hasn't moved. I reach

144

awkwardly across in front of her and gently lift the plate from her hand, which goes limp immediately upon my grasping the weight of the plate. In a fluid motion, Jane melts against me, arms around me, my left hand still awkwardly held over the steel sink, clutching the dripping plate, my right arm sticking out on Jane's other side, holding the damp dishrag. *She must still be holding the green scrubby, but her arms are around me; she must have it pressed against my back.* I carefully set the wet plate down on the counter on the far side of the sink, and pass the towel to my left hand, placing it on the plate, and fold my arms around Jane. She is motionless in my arms, her cheek pressed against my chest, the top of her head by the side of my jaw, almost under my chin.

***

It's one of those moments when we both know perfectly well that we can't hold it forever, but neither of us is willing to make the first move towards ending it. We have probably been standing here for ten minutes, maybe fifteen. After the first couple of minutes, I relaxed into it, my eyes closed, letting the physicality of everything in the room disappear except *Jenny's* Jane's

145

arms around me. Jane isn't sobbing, isn't crying, isn't sniffling or sighing or, in fact, making any sound at all. She is simply wrapped around me, motionless, as motionless as though she were a robe or a coat or a blanket. My hands are on her back, and I am motionless as well; I suspect if I move my hands at all, Jane will think I'm withdrawing. *I know this can't go on forever, and it probably should have stopped already—but not just yet.*

I think about the photo Jane sent, the one that fell out of the letter onto the table when I unsealed the old-fashioned sealing wax from the edges of the folded letter. Falling on the table, in a split second I recognized the photo, knew it instantly although I hadn't seen it in *eight years?* a long time *no, eleven—it's eight since we split up, but I hadn't seen it since shortly after—.* My eyes closed, my arms around Jane, the kitchen gone from my awareness, I trace the image of the photograph in my mind. The edges of our faces are a little blurry—clear enough to see and make us out, but just slightly out of focus. What a photographer would call "soft". Our faces have an orange-yellow appearance, not from the age of the photograph, but from

146

the lighting where it was taken; it was too dark, or the film camera she used did not have fast enough film in it. The edges of the photograph have a dark orangey tinge to them, going into blackish orange darkness. The light was not good, the film speed was wrong, and the focus was soft—but it was the last photo ever taken of Jenny.

Jane abruptly pulls away from me, dabs at her face with her right hand and the back of her wrist *though it didn't sound and now it still doesn't look like she was crying* and absentmindedly sets the green scrubby, still clutched and now crumpled out of shape, onto the back of the steel sink, on a little cracked ceramic soap holder. The green scrubby, released from Jane's grip, immediately stretches out to a crumpled semblance of flatness, and then slowly, imperceptibly, continues to flatten out. *It will flatten out as much as possible, due to minimization of surface tension. As it dries, however, it will likely dry unevenly, and probably the corners at least and maybe one entire side will end up with a concave curl. Like the photograph.*

"You O.K.?"

Jane looks up at me. There is a pause. I'm still standing with my hip against the counter, she's only pulled away a few inches. "I'm O.K." Jane glances around the kitchen. "I could have held you like that for another three hours, but I guess—well, you have work and everything, I'm sure."

I shake my head slightly. "I could have held you for another three hours too, Jane." I take a mincing half step towards her, put my hand on her shoulder. "But I guess I have to let you let me go eventually."

Jane turns away and walks over to the far side of the table, sits down. She's speaking while she walks over: "Then why did you let me go? I could have held on forever." There's almost no tone in her voice. She's sitting down now. "Jesus. That's exactly the problem, isn't it. I'm still holding on, but you let go." She looks intently up at me.

I squint at her. "What are you talking about? I was just holding you. I was—we could have—I mean, I can keep holding you now if you want...?"

"No, I mean—I was—it felt so safe. So secure. And you suddenly—like, pulled away. Like a flinch." Jane rubs a spot on the table, jumps up and retrieves a cloth from by the sink.

She's a foot away from me again. "Jane..."

She glances at me and returns to the table, wiping the spot and then wiping the table around the spot in widening circles. "It's fine, Jack. It's fine." She looks directly at me from the far side of the table. "I can't hold on to you forever." She shakes her head slightly. She opens her mouth as though about to speak again, and then folds her arms on the newly shined table, and lays her head in her arms.

I guess she isn't any less moody than before. I step towards *that's an awful thing to think* the table and *I haven't spoken, hadn't spoken to this woman in at least six years, before this week. I have no idea who she is now. Be generous* stand next to Jane. She doesn't lift her head. I squat down next to her so that my eyes are level with her buried face. I put my hand on her back, at the base of her neck, between her shoulder blades, and rub her back gently and firmly. "Jane..." I'm whispering.

Jane opens an eye *Jenny one eye half open, the morning after the photo* and I resist the

149

urge to stand up; I look at her. "Jane." *I lean over and kiss her on the forehead, and she smiles.* I stand up, bending over at the waist to keep my face nearly level with Jane's, my face rising only a little above hers, and I kiss *Jenny* Jane on the top of her head. *I've missed you.*

I withdraw slowly and Jane tilts her head up at me. "Jack..." *Her voice is dreamy.* She lifts her head and reaches out her hand *she puts her hand on the side of my face, holding my jaw* and hooks her fingers in my collar *reaches out and grasps the steel chain around my neck, pulling me towards her with it* and *looks me dead in the eyes* lifts her head *and lifts her head* and kisses me *and kisses me.*

On the mouth.

Chapter 14

Following Jane *was that just yesterday?* to Perkasie seemed to take forever, the stress of keeping up with her as she wove between cars, around cars, speeding and shuffling and shifting lanes, all the while keeping an eye on the range of my car, which I had not fully charged before meeting her for lunch or brunch or whatever, but coming home from Perkasie, the car fully charged after being plugged in overnight at her house, able to simply punch "Home" on the GPS and casually go with the flow of traffic, seemed to take almost no time at all. I must have been in a daze for most of the ride home, because it seemed that I'd no sooner turned on the PA turnpike than I was turning off it again, halfway home already, barely having noticed. I had some things to figure out.

I can conduct the process with Jane myself. I don't need Karl to run the panel; I can run it. Karl would be better though—he's much more adept at tuning the frequencies, monitoring the subject. I'm better at guiding them verbally and following their conscious or subconscious meanderings, but there is no question that Karl is better at the technical side of things. He is a wizard at it. If I want to help Jane, really help her, help her heal, mentally and, quite possibly, quite probably really, physically, then I will need Karl. I would not be able to provide her with the same level of care, technically speaking. If she were any other client, any high-profile client, there is no way—I would not even consider running her through the process without him. I wouldn't even consider it. If I attempt it—even thinking it, much less suggesting it—it would not be about taking the best care of her, it would be about protecting myself. Because if she is dealing with what I know she is dealing with, she is dealing with what I have not been dealing with, the one thing about our relationship that Karl doesn't know, the thing that will likely—will definitely—come out, if we are effective in the process. If we are effective, it will come out; to be effective necessitates that Karl be there, be involved, be running the control panel and monitoring her brain's wave forms. If Karl is not there, it may not come out, because the process is not effective and we are unable to release everything;

or, it will come out, but not be effective, not be essential. Karl is necessary, if Jane is to heal. The only way to help her is to let the process unfold the way we have designed it, and that means he must be there. That means—he will find out everything.

I pull into the driveway of our house. Amy's at work; I silently power down the vehicle, noticing idly but with gratitude that there is plenty of range to get me to the office, where I can recharge from the site's ample solar power. Inside the house, I go right to the bathroom; though the drive seemed short and the time flew by, I notice that it was over an hour, and I didn't think to urinate before leaving. After relieving myself, I lean on the counter before the mirror. I notice that my shirt is crumpled and my hair, though normally casually untidy, now looks downright unkempt. I lift one arm and sniff my arm pit briefly. *Whew, I'm ripe. I smell like I spent all afternoon having sex and then not showering for the following twenty-four hours.* I glance at my watch; I have time. *I have to get changed anyway; I may as well do it right if I'm going to do it. I don't know who we're working with this afternoon, but I'm sure I shouldn't go in smelling like this.*

I remember that I've set my watch up to download my daily schedule, and I click through the screens until I find the one with the calendar. The type is small and relatively hard to read *not the greatest user interface design* but the layout at least is simple, and I can see that I actually have several hours free; we only have one client, later in the afternoon. A thought strikes me, and I turn and look at the claw foot tub. *I think I'll take a bath.* I haven't taken a bath in I'm not sure how long... *That will be just the ticket. Not optimal for cleaning the body, but the perfect exercise for cleaning the mind.*

Five minutes later I'm lowering myself into the steaming water. I always draw a bath as hot as I can possibly stand it, a habit left over from years of taking a scalding hot bath after a marathon or long training run. I am unused to the heat at first, but I know I will be glad for it after a few minutes, and indeed, a few minutes later, my head lolling back on the high angled ceramic edge of the claw foot tub, submerged to my collarbone in the still very hot (though no longer scalding) water, my sense of time and place slips away. *It is like instant meditation, no effort required. Why haven't*

I been doing this, why has it been so long? My thoughts float dreamily, buoyed by the steaming water and floating away in the misty mindset that overcomes me. I absentmindedly brush my chest and underarms, up and down my legs, and my crotch, with the hot water, not using soap or any other products, same as is my habit in the shower; I don't scrub, but lazily let the piercing warmth of the water be disturbed by the motion of my hands into freshly assaulting my skin. The heat flutters over me in waves matching the waves created by my hands, but I am almost completely unaware; my mind is floating in its own bath, heated by the thoughts of a day ago and a decade ago, mixed together, pulsing against each other as we'd pulsed against each other, as the heat of the water is pulsing against my skin, red, flushed, invisibly sweating in the shimmering heat of the water and the memories.

Chapter 15

I amble casually into the office; Karl's in the control room already. *He loves to be over-prepared.* I'm setting down my satchel and he bursts out. "Where've you been?"

After my hot bath and relaxing afternoon, after the emotionally tumultuous thirty hours prior to the bath, I am feeling very mellow, and the tone in Karl's voice startles me. *He sounds annoyed.* "What do you mean?" I briefly panic, thinking perhaps I'd missed an appointment this morning or even yesterday afternoon—but no, I'd double-checked. The next appointment was not until this afternoon, and we wouldn't be expecting the client for almost an hour.

"Dude." Karl's voice is not raised, but there is an edginess to it that makes me uncomfortable. *He's usually so easy-going. Am I reading too much into this? Projecting that his mental state is somehow mimicking the mercuriality of my own this week? I'll have to be careful about that.* "You're late." Karl squints at me. "Are you O.K.?" He pauses. "You're never late." *The edginess seems to have softened; he sounds concerned.*

I shake my head. "What do you mean?" I glance at my watch; it's only 15:07, and the client isn't due to even arrive until 16:00. "We have almost an hour...."

Karl shakes his head and claps me on the shoulder, kindly, wrapping his arm around me and guiding me into the control room. "Good thing they're in—no one saw you wander casually in like that. Jesus." He opens the heavy door of the control room and gestures for me to go ahead. I enter in front of him, and he's talking from behind me before we can sit down. "Why do you have that fancy watch if you never look at it, man?"

I can't tell if he's annoyed or just repeating a refrain. "What do you mean? I *did* look at it." I glance down again. It's only 15:08. *I just looked; of course it's only been a minute.*

Karl chuckles. We're standing by the control panels, the screens and dials on the heavy table, and Karl reaches his hands out to me. I stand motionless for a moment before realizing that I'm wearing my coat.

It's relatively warm out, for November, but my car gets better range if I don't run the heat, so I sometimes wear it if I think it might be chilly in the evening. I doff my woolen coat *Jenny gave me this coat; she found it at an Army-Navy store somewhere. It has the name of the Marine it was issued to sewn into the inside. I love this coat. She knew I would* and hand it to Karl, who turns swiftly and hangs it on the hanger behind the door. He turns back and fixes me with a steady look; a smile creeps across his face. "Do not disturb, right?" He arches an eyebrow at me.

"Huh?"

"You must've put your fancy watch on 'Do not disturb' mode again. And then forgotten about it—again." I click the button on my watch and note that I had indeed left it on 'Do Not Disturb'. *I'll need that on anyway for our upcoming session, so I'll leave it for now.* I look up at Karl, who shakes his head and chuckles. "Absent-minded genius, much?" He claps the side of my arm jovially. "You're a piece of work dude." He turns and sits down quickly. "Let's get this checklist stuff done. They're still settling in, but they *have* been waiting a bit."

I blink at Karl. *Oh, I get it.* "You changed the schedule."

Karl points at me without looking up, his pointer finger extended. "Bingo, genius." He types rapidly on the keyboard in front of him. "C'mon, let's get going. Check your equipment." I sit down and scootch my chair closer to the table. "It should be fine— I skimmed through your checklist while I was waiting for you, but you'll want to double-check."

I stifle a giggle. "Yeah, you can say that again. We don't need another 'Prima Donna' situation." *The time I had skimped on the checklist and we had an equipment failure with a client who was a well-known actress. She was actually very gracious about it, but we were afraid she'd be a prima donna and we'd have problems. That was early on, but we referred to it in times like these.*

"No, sir. Especially not with the big boss."

I glance over at Karl. "The big boss?"

He looks over at me, pausing in his typing. "Yeah, you know. His suit costs more than your car."

I smile at Karl. "For the price you gave me, a lot of things cost more than my car."

"O.K. well each of his shoes probably costs more than your car, how's that." He turns to the keyboard and types a series of commands rapidly, seemingly forcefully. "O.K." He shoves the keyboard off and to the side, clicks something on one of his screens with the mouse. "I'm set." He swivels and looks at me. I'm running my finger along a line of ready lights; I glance briefly at him and continue my checklist. "Look, I didn't mean to be gruff back there, when you came in."

I glance back at Karl and smirk. "If that's you being gruff then I have no problems until you get maybe homocidal. Then you might come off as slightly rude."

"Well, thanks."

"No, it's cool. I mean, you're always super cool man. I figured something was up, given that you seemed rushed, but you certainly weren't gruff or anything."

I glance over and catch Karl nodding. *He looks much more relaxed.* "They called this morning. Big Boss's plane got in early, or they took an early plane, or something. Wanted to push it up two hours."

"Two hours? Oh, jeez, man, I'm sorry." I've stopped and am looking at him.

Karl raises his eyes. "If you're sorry about accidentally being an hour late, the best way to make it up to me is actually *not* to stop what you're doing...."

I smirk and continue my checklist. "I'm almost done anyway."

"I know, I see where you're at." *Karl designed the checklist; he knows it better than I do.* "Yeah, so I updated the schedule, with an alert to you. This morning, when it happened. But *you*—" he gets up and walks over, stands behind my chair, starts rubbing my shoulders, my trapezius. "*You* clearly had *other* things on your mind, eh?" He slaps my back collegiately. "Eh, champ?" He retrieves his chair and slides it over nearer mine and sits down.

I finish the last item, take one more look down the checklist, and turn away from the controls. Karl adopts a mock-serious face. "Am I to presume that things went—ahem—*well* with your ex-wife?"

I stare at his comically straight face. "Former wife."

"Excuse me. Former wife." He straightens up, if possible, even more. "So...?"

I nod.

The corners of Karl's mouth twitch, and he bursts into a grin. "Jesus, man, you really are a lady killer." I stare at him; an electric-tingly burst of adrenaline just shot down my back and I can feel my limbs tingling, but Karl is still talking, "...in my life. Seriously. Doesn't matter how much you put her through, or she put you through, or anything." He shakes his head. "Last week you're so emotional about even *hearing* from her that I have to take you out for dinner and give you the afternoon off." He holds up his hand, silencing me. "And I know—I know. We didn't have anything scheduled that afternoon anyway, and also I'm not your boss, I'm just your measly fifty percent partner. So I guess you could have taken the afternoon off anyway. Or maybe, depending on how you look at it, you weren't required to be working to begin with." He lowers his hand into a pointing finger. "That's not my point, though."

"I've lost track man. What exactly *is* your point?"

"My point," Karl jabs his pointer finger in my direction, "is that you are a wizard, my friend."

"A wizard?"

"Well, I was gonna say 'lady killer' again, but when I said that a minute ago, you looked like I farted in church, and I know, I know, in our business we need to mind our language, and you wouldn't want to be thought of by anyone as actually killing any ladies." *I feel nauseated.* "But no, you're a wizard. You go from being Mr. Mopey Pants to Mr. Takes Off Her Pants, in what, two days?"

I look steadily at him, and clear my throat. "Three. I think it had been three days since I got the letter. Four, now."

Karl leans forward, his eyes twinkling. "The error that proves my point." He makes a motion with his mouth, as though he's licking his lips, only he's not; he sort of rolls his lips against each other. "So, I'm not wrong about the pants."

I try to think of something clever to say, but my mind is bouncing between the conversation we're having now and the conversation we'll be having after Jane does the process. *Lady killer.* After what seems like a long time of Karl leaning maniacally forward towards me, I spread my hands in surrender. "What can I say?" Karl leans back, victorious. "That girl always had good taste."

Karl throws his head back and starts to howl with laughter but stifles it quickly, his hand over his mouth. I'm confused for a moment and then realize something.

"Karl. Is the big boss in there waiting for us?" Karl is giggling into his hand as he nods at me. "I thought I was running like an hour late?"

Karl shakes his head. "Nah man, I'm just messing with you. We still have like half an hour."

I stare at Karl. "You..."

"Don't say it!"

I squeeze my lips together and shake my head. I laugh. "Alright man. You got me."

Karl nods. "That's right. Now," he pats my leg affectionately. "You gonna give a brother some details, or what?" His eyes are sparkling again.

I shake my head. "Actually, there is one thing about our—ahem—encounter, that I ought to talk to you about." Karl's eyes are gleaming. *Let's see how this goes.*

***

After I explain to Karl that Jane wants to do the process, he's just sitting there looking at me. "So..."

"So...?"

"So, what do you think?" I'm looking at him, expectantly.

"What do I think about what?"

I scrunch my face at him. "Do you think—I mean, can we, uh—fit her in?" Karl starts to speak but I hold up my hand. "I'm being serious, now. Do you think that we can schedule her to do the process?"

Karl looks dubiously at me. "What are you talking about?"

I'm confused. "She—she wants to—"

"Dude, I know. You just spent—" Karl glances back at the door where there's a large digital clock over the transom. "You just spent *ten* minutes telling me, basically, that your ex—excuse me, your former wife would like to do the process, because she's all fucked up about what happened with you guys, and she thinks it'll help her beat cancer." He pauses. "Is that basically right?"

I nod. "Yeah. You've got it."

"And now..." Karl purses his lips and smiles. "Now you're sitting there with a sad puppy look on your face, asking me if I think we could maybe, possibly, just this once, hopefully, do you think, just maybe, if only —schedule her?"

I'm staring at Karl. "Yeah, basically. I mean, I know you don't do the actual scheduling, but—"

Karl cuts me off with a whoop of laughter. He throws his head back and then leans forward and stomps one foot on the floor. He slaps his thigh, and when I start to say something, he holds up his hand. He's practically wheezing as he reins in his laughing. "Dude, you really are a piece of work!"

I'm not sure what's so funny here. "I'm not sure what's so funny, actually. I just thought that maybe—I mean, it's sort of a special situation..." *I can feel myself being defensive. Relax.*

"Jack—" Karl stops laughing abruptly and looks at me, his face serious, composed, but stern. "What kind of operation do you think we're running here? We have *top* people— the big boss guy is gonna be here any minute—and you want me to, what? Go talk to Martha and just tell her to shove some high-rollers aside, because you worked your wizard magic on your—ahem, former partner?"

I look down at my hands in my lap. "I guess I just thought," quietly.

"Jesus, man!" Karl has leapt up from his chair and is squatting in front of me, in view of my downcast head. He grips underneath my chin and lifts my head up as he stands up. "Dude—I'm just playing with you." He squints at me, still holding underneath my chin. "*Are* you O.K.? I know you were—you were pretty fucked up yourself when you guys split up." He pauses. "Ever since—well, ever since your sister, frankly." I feel my mouth twitch. "Hey—" he releases my chin, reaches behind himself to grasp his chair and move it forward to sit in it, right in front of me. "I'm just playing with you man. Of *course* we can fit her in. She was your *wife*, man. I don't know what counts as a special case if that doesn't."

I let out a breath I didn't realize I'd been holding. I take in a deep breath and let it out in a sigh. I shake my head. "Dude..."

"Don't even say it."

"Say what—what was I going to say?"

Karl fixes me with a look, the corners of his mouth already twitching. "That I make you crazy sometimes."

I raise my eyebrows at him. "And why shouldn't I say it?"

"Because," he's now grinning again, "in order for me to make you crazy *sometimes*, you would have to, presumably, be *not* crazy at least sometimes—and you, sir, are a *loon!*" He is grinning triumphantly, and I can feel tears in my eyes. "Jesus, man, I'm just kidding. What's the matter?"

I shake my head and wipe my eyes with the back of my wrist. "No, it's O.K." He's still looking at me. "I'll tell you later; totally unrelated." I take another deep breath. "I guess I have been a little on edge with this whole Jane business. It's a lot, you know?" Karl nods. "So you don't think that it'll be a big deal?"

Karl half-smirks. "Dude, I'll literally just ring Martha and tell her we have a special case. Just find out from Jane what day works for her. It's no big deal, I'm sure. We do it all the time for big wigs."

I nod. "Hey." Karl looks at me. "Thanks, man."

Karl looks bemused. "It's *really* not a big deal man." He stands up and pushes his chair in under the control table. "Besides—" he glances at the large clock and heads over to the door, opens it and half-exits, then turns back and pops his head around the thick door. "I can barely wait to hear all the juicy stuff she shares about you!" He winks and disappears to go wait for the client.

You have no idea, man.

Chapter 16

The process with the big boss was nothing out of the ordinary. One of his assistants, while we were getting him wired in, mentioned that they'd hoped to move the appointment forward two hours, because of some flight situation, but they understood how very busy we were. Karl kept a straight face, which amazed me somewhat, and explained that we were often booked months in advance, which is true. The assistant seemed flustered that an exception could not have been made, but the big boss dismissed the whole thing. *He* seemed pleased to be involved with an operation as notoriously, if not infamously, private and yet over-booked as us. I kept my mouth shut, but I caught Karl eyeballing me, and it looked like he winked, but I looked away quickly. *As practiced as I am, as many hours as I've spent controlling my emotional reactions, that guy can crack me up in two seconds flat. This is not a good time.*

By the time we finish a few hours later, upload the appropriate files for post-processing and analysis, and I make it back out to the car, it's dark out. *Getting dark early these days; it's just past 18:00 but it's already fully night time.* I clutch the wool pea coat around me—not yet in the habit of buttoning it up before going outside—against the *surprisingly chilly* wind, and dash over to my car, which is only a few dozen feet away, since the electric-car-only parking spots are premier spots, close to the building. My hands are chilly by the time I disconnect the charger and get in the car; I'll leave the cabin heat off, but the steering wheel itself is heated, and it's already warming up. I'm pleased to notice that the few hours I was inside was enough to charge the car back to full battery, as full as the battery would get at its age, anyway.

It's only a couple minutes' drive home, but my hands are warmed up in that time, and I notice Amy's car in the driveway when I turn onto our street. Amy tends to park nearer the center of the driveway than the side, but I don't mind; I feel more comfortable about my ability to pull in safely next to her car than in her ability to pull in safely next to mine. *Not that I would care if she nicked my car, but I'm sure she would be upset about it. I like a car that comes pre-banged up a bit—saves me the worry.*

Amy is sitting on the couch in the living room, her feet up *slippers that she wears outside up on the couch*. She's reading, and there is some detritus of a recently consumed meal on the little table next to her: plate, seltzer can, and a crumpled napkin. I am about to open my mouth to say something, I'm actually in the process of opening my mouth, and Amy holds up one hand, then extends her pointer finger vertically. *One minute.* I close my mouth and stand impotently waiting; I set my satchel down by the couch and am about to exit the room to find something for myself in the kitchen when *I'm actually not that hungry* Amy folds closed her book, thumbs inside holding her place, resting it on her lap as she flings her head backwards on the cushioned arm of the couch, closing her eyes and exclaiming passionately, "Oh my *God* this is a good book." She lifts her head and her *green, like Jenny's* eyes flash at me. "Jack, you *must* read this book. I'm telling you—you'd love it!"

I stare at Amy for a moment, and then sit down at the far end of the couch. "Well," Amy shoots me a look, and I pause *maybe I shouldn't say anything* before continuing, "I *don't* like when you blaspheme."

"Oh, *Jesus*, Jack, give me a break!" Amy removes one hand from her book, keeping the other, thumb inside, still holding her place, tightly gripped as she swats my leg with the book. "Lighten up." She says this nicely, playfully; there's a playful tone in her voice. "I figured you'd be in a better mood after being—" she leans forward mischievously "out *all night...*" I squint at Amy and she holds the book with both hands and makes a gyrating motion with her shoulders and the extended book, singing "allll niiigght looong...." followed by an imitation of an instrument "doo doodoo doo doo..."

I smile. *I guess I didn't have anything to worry about with Amy. In the end I wasn't sure if she'd even notice. But of course she noticed. And of course she doesn't care. She's a good kid.* "Hey, knock it off."

"What're you—tired?" Amy scootches up from against the couch arm, briefly opens her book and looks at the page number, then twists around and sets the book on the end table behind her, somehow finding a place for it between the plate, the seltzer can, the napkin, and the lamp. She whips around and folds her *slippers on the couch* feet under her legs, sitting in the position I grew up calling "indian style" but which she grew up calling "criss-cross apple sauce", since the world had already moved on in the years between the two of us attending kindergarten.

She's looking at me with *big green* eyes wide open, expectantly. After a moment of neither of us saying anything, she cocks her head to the side slightly and raises an eyebrow at me. "So, are you gonna tell your baby sister how it worked out with the ex?" I open my mouth and she holds up her hand. "Nope!" I close my mouth. "Say no more!" I smile, bemused. She smiles at me. "Your silence," she lowers her voice huskily, "last night..." and in a normal voice, "tells me *everything* I need to know!"

"Amy..."

"Jack, wait:" she holds out her hand in a "stop" gesture. "One more thing..."

"What?"

"*Former.*"

"Former?"

"Yes!" She titters *adorably.* "I know, I shouldn't call her your 'ex' wife, I should call her your 'former' wife, but I said 'the ex', and not 'the ex wife', so I should have said, 'the *former*', as in: 'How did it go staying over last night with your *former*?'"

I stare at Amy for a moment, and then smile, shake my head, and look down at my hands for a moment. "You—you are quite pleased with yourself, aren't you?"

Amy holds her arms out to the sides; she holds her left arm out over the floor, and her right arm she holds over the back of the couch, drawn in slightly so as not to hit the window as it would if it were fully extended; she gives a little bow in place. "Hey, you're the one who should be proud of himself. I'm merely clever. You are the *lady killer.*" She fixes me with a look and *electric spikes down my back again* bursts out laughing. "So, how did it go?" and she's resting her chin in her hands, elbows leaning on her thighs, big green eyes wide open, waiting to hear what I'm willing to

178

share with her about the time I spent with Jane.

Chapter 17

"Look," I'm looking at her, her eyes batting coquettishly at me, "I'm happy to tell you all about it—"

"*All* about it? Will you really tell me *all* about it, you dirty thing?" She's put her hand on my thigh, by my knee. I'm sitting indian style now, too.

"Amy," I swat her hand. "Knock it off..."

"O.K., O.K., you can skip the dirtiest parts—not like I'd want to hear that kinda thing with my brother, sheesh." She mock shivers. My cheek twitches. "Although..."

"Although what?"

She bats her eyes a bit again, and leans over. Her voice is lowered, actually lowered, not fake-husky like before. "I won't tell if you won't tell, if you tell."

I blink. "Wait, what?"

She straightens back up and shrugs her shoulders, looking off to either side, frowning a bit, nonchalantly. "I'm just saying—we're both adults. We're housemates." She glances up at me briefly. "I'm your sister—" looking away now "but if I were just some chick you shared the rent with..." Her voice trails off. "Would you tell me all the filthy details then?" She looks at me again, arching her eyes, before looking down at her hands in her lap. "Anyway, you *know* I haven't been out 'all night' in—well, Jesus, a while anyway."

I squint at her, but she's still looking down at her hands. "What do you mean?"

"Jesus, Jack, do I have to spell it out for you?" Now she's looking at me again, and there's a strained look in her face. *Straining to get me to understand? To get out what she's trying to say, maybe.* She quickly shrugs again and looks nowhere in particular. Her voice is pointedly jovial. "I guess, at this point, I'll take whatever excitement I can get." She contorts her face into a "why not?" look: a forced half-frown, arched eyebrows; I can almost hear her saying, "What the hell?" She glances up at me and then quickly down at her lap.

"Amy..."

"Hm?"

"O.K., listen. I—" she looks up at me suddenly, piercingly, startlingly; I'm startled, and I forget what I was going to say *big green eyes next thing you know she'll say "We're both grown-ups now, Jack."*

"What...? Too much...?"

"No, not that." I've recovered myself.

"Because, I mean—" she fixes me with a stare, intently. "We're both grown-ups, Jack." *Jesus.* I swallow and I'm suddenly aware of the placement my limbs, of my skin underneath my clothing. *My blood is flowing.* "I think we're old enough to—to talk about anything we want to." She's still looking at me, but her face softens. "I mean, not that you have to—you don't have to tell me anything." She reaches out and puts her hand on my knee. "Jesus, Jack, I mean I'm just—I'm mostly just playing with you." *Maybe I look the way I feel at the moment. I wish she she hadn't said "lady killer" earlier—same thing Karl said.* She gives a short, small laugh. "I mean, you don't have to tell me *any*thing, *any*thing at all."

I shake my head and take her hand off my knee and hold it in mine *exactly the way Jane held my hand at the table yesterday. Or was that this morning?* "Amy," I smile. "I know." She nods. "Look, I don't mind— you're right, we're both—" I force myself to keep talking continuously "grown-ups and" *I don't think she noticed me pause* "we can talk about whatever kinds of things that roommates or housemates or whatever talk about." Now I pause. "There's just one thing..."

Amy's eyes had perked up while I was talking, and now she gives me a suspicious look. "Oh...? What's that...?"

I resettle myself, still holding her hand, and straighten up, and look at her with my best gesture of authority without sternness. "Before I give you all the filthy details of my overnight stay with my, ah, *former*." She smiles. "I have a request."

There's a pause. "What is it?" *She sounds breathless.*

"I request," I am measuring my words, "and I really mean this. I request that you please, *please*, pretty please, with pickles on top—"

"Oh Jesus Christ, Jack—"

I close my eyes and tilt my head to the side disapprovingly. "Yes, thank you. Exactly my point. Would you *please*, pretty please, stop blaspheming?" She looks like she's about to say something and I squeeze her hand gently. I do my best impression of her *mesmerizing green* big-eyed cute look. "Seriously. Please?"

Amy pauses, her mouth compressed, her eyes scalding. She pulls her hand away from mine and leans back, then abruptly stands up. She turns and forcefully grabs the dish, can, and napkin from the little table behind the arm of the couch, saying, "Fine." She whips around and points the empty seltzer can at me. "But you'd better *spill* with those details, you self-righteous..."

"Don't say it!"

She cuts herself off from saying the word *bastard, I'm sure* and clamps her lips shut. She's standing over the couch, looking down at me. She takes two steps towards the kitchen; I'm turning my head, watching her walk away. She stops dead still and looks down at me. "*Spill*." I raise my eyebrows at her, and she raises hers at me, comically, and races out of the living room to dispose of her items.

***

When Amy returns to the living room, she hands me a pint of ice cream and a spoon. *It's the big heavy spoon she knows is my favorite.* "What's this?" I notice she's holding another pint and spoon as she settles herself down at the opposite end of the couch.

She tilts her head and eyeballs me as she peels the lid off her carton. "Um, it's ice cream." She fiddles with the plastic liner underneath the cardboard lid and mutters, "Some genius..." before whipping it off in a smooth, fast motion. She looks up at me, holding my ice cream pint and spoon, foolishly. "You open the top, here," she holds up the cardboard lid, still clutched in the hand now holding the plastic film, "this is called the 'lid', and if you don't take it off first, it makes the ice cream harder to eat." She purses her lips at me.

"Ha ha. Very funny. What I meant was—"

"And *whence* you remove the lid, there is another—" she lowers her voice to a whisper "*secret* lid, made out of plastic."

She raises her voice to normal volume. "You have to peel that one off, too, or else—you guessed it—hard to eat your ice cream."

"Amy—"

"Tut tut tut." She waves the hand holding the lids, cardboard and plastic, at me. I don't move and she waves her hand again. I smile and sigh and remove the cardboard lid to my ice cream, and she turns and puts her two lids, cardboard and plastic, on the little table behind her, on the other side of the arm of the couch. She watches me as I fumble with the small edge of the plastic film. "That's it—see? It's tricky." When I peel it off, she exclaims, "Now you've got it!"

"O.K. goofball." I wait, and she doesn't say anything, just looks at me expectantly. "What?"

"I was waiting to see if you knew what to do next."

"Um, I assume that I use this little shovel-like device to scoop some of the—what did you call it again?"

"Ice cream." She's beaming.

"Some of the ice cream out of the little container ad into my mouth." I raise my eyebrows at her. "Is that right?"

"Nope!" She wiggles around in excitement at her end of the couch.

I'm genuinely confused. "It's not?" I hold the pint of ice cream up to eye level and look at it. "Here I thought I understood the general theory of ice cream..."

Amy laughs. "Well, this is a special case." She settles back against the arm of the couch. "This isn't actually ice cream, or normal ice cream anyway. It's some kind of low carb high protein stuff that *someone* suggested I try out."

She's looking at me. *I don't remember telling her anything about buying low-carb ice cream.* "Um, O.K., so what, it's not actually edible?" *I think I'm being funny.*

She smiles. "You have to let it sit for a few minutes." She's staring at me, squinting. "It doesn't have the same crap in it as regular ice cream, so it freezes hard as a rock. If you let it sit for five minutes, it's better. It's actually surprisingly like ice cream at that point."

I wait, but she says no more, just looks at me. "O.K." *She is still looking at me.* I hold the ice cream pint; my hand is getting cold. "How long—five minutes? My hand is getting cold."

"Well, put it down, silly." She impales her spoon into her pint, wedging it, I notice, in between the cardboard side and the frozen center, and sets the carton on the floor next to the couch. She raises her eyebrows at me and I follow suit, though I first try to shove the spoon into the center of the ice cream itself; she's right—it's frozen completely solid, and so I wedge my spoon in between the solid mass and the cardboard side, which flexes out of the way enough for my spoon to easily lodge there. I place mine on the floor and look back up at Amy.

"You didn't answer my question, though."

"Didn't I?" *She's being awfully mischievous tonight.*

"No, you didn't."

"Oh, sorry, Jackie." She pouts. "What was your question that I didn't answer?"

"My question is, what's with the ice cream?"

"Fake, low-carb ice cream substitute, Mr. Precise."

I roll my eyes. "O.K., what's with the fake, low-carb ice cream substitute? I haven't even had dinner yet." *Not that I'm hungry.*

Amy leans over towards me. When I don't move, she wags a finger in a "come hither" motion. I lean forward, and she's speaking low, conspiratorially. "You may not know this, *Jack*, but when girlfriends get together and talk about the men they're—" she lowers her voice further, and in an exaggerated hoarse whisper, "*having sex with*" She pauses and licks her lips *jesus god help me, I can feel my blood* and continues in a low voice, "they often like to have a little something-something to go with the conversation. A treat." She leans back against her side of the couch. "And the best treat to have, when there's some really juicy story, is the pint—" she reaches to the floor and swiftly retrieves her pint carton, "of gourmet ice cream." She looks down and experimentally fiddles with the spoon against the *apparently still frozen* block of ice cream, then sets the carton back down on the floor. "Of course, in this case, we're having gourmet fake low-carb high-protein, fake ice cream." She shrugs. "But it's what we have."

I nod. "O.K., so you brought us ice cream so that—uh, I can tell you about, about Jane?" She nods. "Like we're—like we're, ah, girlfriends?"

She nods her head emphatically. "Precisely!"

I smile. "O.K." *I'll tell you whatever you want to know, about Jane, about me and Jane, this time. Today, and yesterday, as long as I don't have to tell you about eleven years ago, or you'll never bring me ice cream and make jokes with me again.*

Chapter 18

By the time our ice creams are soft enough
to eat, I've started telling Amy about
meeting Jane for brunch. I tell her about
the nice time we had, catching up, and how
we both seemed to avoid getting into any
heavy topics. As I'm explaining it to Amy, I
realize that I really did enjoy being with
Jane yesterday morning. It surprises me,
not because I didn't enjoy the ensuing
twenty-four hours of being with her, but
simply because, as I now realize, I was so
focused yesterday on everything being
alright that I didn't actually pay attention to
how much I was enjoying just being with
her. It was as though the unvoiced mutual
agreement to not discuss anything
significant took away any pressure, and we
were able to just *be* with one another, and I
liked it. I definitely still find her attractive,
and it's been long enough since everything
that happened that I was able, yesterday,
and afterwards, to partition it, most of the
time, the most of the time that we spent not
talking about anything, to partition it away,
and just enjoy first the simply being

together, and then the resurgence of the attraction, and then...

"And when I got into the car, I was sitting there for a minute, thinking about it, and—"

Amy pauses, holding her spoon in her mouth after having sucked the mouthful of ice cream from it. With a swift move she yanks the spoon out of her mouth, sucking on it on the way out to extract the last bit of ice cream from that spoonful. Her lips follow the movement of the spoon, pulled out after it by the motion of the retracting spoon and the suction they're exerting on it, and she smacks her lips softly when the spoon is fully removed; she points the bowl of the spoon at me and purses her lips, squinting at me, forming her words. "You—no! *She* called *you*, right? No—" She puts the spoon back in her mouth and sucks on it for another moment, squinting at me. Suddenly she yanks the spoon out of her mouth; free of further suction, it is surprisingly fast, and she wags the bowl at me again. "She *texted* you, right?" I nod, and Amy digs her spoon into her pint carton, saying as if to herself, "Knew it!" She lifts the spoonful to her mouth and raises her eyebrows at me. "Well?" She pops the spoon into her mouth and extracts it, mostly free of the ice cream, and says, her mouth opening wide around the fresh mouthful of ice cream, "Go on..." She reinserts the spoon and sucks on it meditatively, watching me.

I'm getting to the part where she sticks her hand down my pants. I'm not sure how much of this I should say. I fish another spoonful of ice cream from my carton, stalling. Amy is eyeballing me, and I know she knows I'm stalling. I start to tell her about being in the car and how anxious I was trying to follow Jane on the highway— what it was like and the range of the car and everything, and partway through my story, Amy throws her head back and practically shouts, "Oh... my... God!" She levels her gaze at me. "Jack. Jack, honey." She starts to say something else, and then focuses on digging out another scoop of ice cream. She raises the loaded spoon and glances at it, down at the carton, and at me. "Jackie, I don't know about you, but I'm like a third through this pint and you haven't even gotten back to her place yet. Give your little sister a break would you?" She sucks the ice cream off the spoon and again talks around it. "C'mon..." She swallows. "I'm going to revoke your ice cream privileges.

Let's get to it. You got to her house. Did you go right up to bed or did you beat around the bush?" When I don't say anything for a moment, she pouts and looks down into her carton. Her voice is quiet. "You would've told Jenny I bet." It's not accusatory, it's simply stated. She sounds sad, in fact, but it still startles me *upsets me* somewhat. *Of course I'd tell Jenny. Jenny already knows—knew—everything. Almost everything.*

I'm staring at *my little sister* Amy, and I swallow. "Actually..." Her eyes widen slightly. I clear my throat. *I can feel my blood.* "When we got to her place—she was pretty much all over me." I pause; she's watching me. "We pretty much got right to it."

Amy smiles demurely and fishes out another spoonful. When I don't continue, she arches her eyebrows while scraping out a large dollop. "And...?" She sucks off part of the large dollop, leaving a smooth concave portion clinging to the spoon.

I shake my head. "And..." *now or never* "and, we fucked, pretty much, right away." Amy is nodding. *That wasn't so hard.* "For like two hours."

196

Amy snorts or chortles or something; she unceremoniously whips the spoon from her mouth, covering her mouth with her hand. She seems to be trying to swallow and avoid choking, and she succeeds after a moment of intense concentration, followed by an exploding laugh. She's nodding and smiling. "Nice..." She nods and seems to think about it. "Two hours continuously?" She shifts around in place, adjusting her position without really moving, moving her thighs up and down and wiggling her butt in place, still sitting cross-legged at the end of the couch, and ending up in what looks like the exact same position.

"No, I mean—" *I guess I'm in it now. We're friends—just think of it as being friends.* "Well, we did it for like an hour, I guess. Then fell asleep—"

"*You* fell asleep or *you both* fell asleep?"

"Uh, we both did." I pause, reflecting. "I mean, I think we both did. I was asleep, I know that much. I suppose I can't actually know for sure that she was asleep. I mean, I assume she was asleep because otherwise she would have moved around and woken me up, but I seemed to wake up gradually after a while. What?" Amy is smirking. *She was just making fun of me.* "Oh."

She laughs, then, extending one of her folded legs, kicks my leg softly with her foot, just with the toes. "Go on, silly. I'm just playing with you." She sucks another concave clinging portion of ice cream from her spoon, the bowl of the spoon facing towards her, her scooping the ice cream off with her tongue; she's batting her eyes at me, and she smacks her lips. "Continue telling me how you spent all afternoon yesterday fucking your former while some of us were busy working at our actual jobs..." She's finished slurping the ice cream from the spoon and is looking at the concave side of the bowl of the spoon, thoughtfully. "Not getting any action. Fucking zero-many people. Unlike some people who spent all afternoon..." She seems to shudder, closes her eyes and shivers almost, then opens her eyes wide, looking at me. She's tapping the tip of the bowl of the spoon on her lower lip, which is hanging slightly open, and jutting out.

I shake my head and smile, forcing a smile which then becomes genuine; I have a thought. "Hey, what can I say?" I retrieve a small spoonful. "Nice work if you can get

198

it!" I pop it in my mouth, and she mock glares at me. "So, yeah, we woke up after an hour, and... I guess we were both still feeling it."

"So you fucked for another hour?" Amy taps her spoon on the top edge of her carton. "Jeez, give the poor girl some rest." She fixes me with a steady gaze. "Or are you gonna claim that she was 'all over you' again, Mr. Casanova-man."

I shake my head and smile.

***

Once I got over the initial reticence about talking about everything with Amy, it was fairly straightforward. She'd made a couple pointed remarks, and I did too, but I think we were sort of both pointedly being crude to sort of get it out of the way, and once we'd both made a point of it, the conversation was very natural. I told her about how Jane had made me dinner, how I had mixed feelings about it. I told her about how nice it was and how confusing and *I didn't tell her how I was thinking of Jenny the whole time* how I eventually told Jane about the work Karl and I do. I told her that Jane was going to do the process, and how I felt that it would really help her to get things off her chest. Amy was quiet, watching me. I think she was thinking about how she'd told me how she blamed Jane, and maybe she was thinking that it would help her to get some things off her chest, too.

I didn't tell her what I was carrying around, but *at some point maybe I should. Maybe it's possible to...* I kept thinking, as I was explaining to Amy how Jane was going to do the process, and how I thought it would benefit her, I kept thinking how *I will have to do it, and I will have to trust that Karl will understand.* Karl will understand. *And then maybe I too can put the whole thing behind me.*

Chapter 19

Karl messages me later that night, letting me know that Marsha or Martha or whatever-her-name-is that does the scheduling shifted some things around, and Jane is scheduled for the day after tomorrow, as long as that still works for her. I message him back thanking him, and let her know *Marsha or Martha. I really should remember which is which* that I and Jane greatly appreciate it, and I send a text to Jane letting her know. *It's not like it's that big of a company, but it's hardly my fault. We have both a Marsha and a Martha, and they're both middle-aged women of about the same age, height, build, and hair color. And I'm pretty sure they switched jobs at one point, so the one that does it now is not the one who used to do it. But maybe I'm making that up. I think Martha is the one who does the scheduling now, and Marsha is in billing or whatever. This was easier when it was just Karl and me booking everything ourselves. Of course, we didn't have any money then, and I was still working part-time as a professor. I suppose I have it better now...* I fall asleep.

***

It's two days later, the day after tomorrow. I meet Jane in the parking lot. I'm standing by my car *it really is unseasonably warm for November. I brought my wool coat that Jenny bought me, but it must be over sixty degrees out right now* and she glances at the thick wire plugged into the front. "Plugging in already?" She's making eyes at me. "I didn't realize that was part of your 'process', but I mean—I'm open-minded."

I scoff and smile and extend my hand in the direction of the building entrance. It's only a couple dozen yards away, and she gives me a look but then steps brightly up onto the curb and starts walking towards the door.

Inside, one of the Marthas greets us. "Good afternoon, Ms. Peterson." *It hadn't occurred to me that she'd gone back to her maiden name. I don't know why it hadn't occurred to me. Not that it matters. It doesn't matter. But I would have thought that she would have mentioned it at some point.* Jane glances at me quickly, and I avert my eyes. "I'm Martha Shields, we spoke on the phone yesterday." *Ah ha! So it is Martha. I wonder if they're actually both named Martha? Maybe I imagined that there was a Marsha at all?*

Martha is extending her hand, and Jane is shaking hands with her and saying something pleasant, when Karl bursts into the room from the door in the side of the back wall, the one with the hallway leading to the control room. *As opposed to the bathroom door. This is a pretty small office considering the kind of business that we do.* "Jane!" Karl leans down and gives Jane a hug, and they kiss on each cheek. He's grinning, and she's smiling, too. "*So* nice to see you!" He glances around; Martha and I are standing idly, and he flicks his head in my direction. "This one I see nine days a week..." I smile and glance at Jane. *She looks happy.* "But, gosh—I didn't know if I'd ever run into you again. It is nice to see you." Karl catches himself and his face moves slightly. He lowers his voice. "I mean, under the circumstances, though..."

Jane shakes her head swiftly. I notice that she and Karl are holding both each others' hands. "No, no, it's fine." She clears her throat. "I mean, *I'm* fine. Just a little mental cleaning needed, you know how it is..."

Karl releases Jane's hands and turns, steps back and makes a sweeping gesture to include me, Martha, Martha's desk, the funny potted palm tree, and the rest of the little front office. "Well, you've come to the right place. Behold!" His gesture is comically grand in the small space, and we all smile. *That's Karl for you. Always the comedian. He told me once that laughter is the best medicine for the soul, and he means it.*

Jane is nodding. "That's what I understand." She elbows me. "You know, Karl—*this one* almost didn't tell me what you two are up to these days." Karl opens his mouth in an exaggerated "O" of horror. "I'm not sure if he was just trying to keep the business a secret, or just didn't want me to see you again." She bats her eyes at Karl, who almost giggles.

"My love, you know I adore you, but even if you are no longer Jack's lady, you are—and I mean this with great respect—not my kind of lady." Jane laughs. *Well at least she seems comfortable enough. That's good. For her. I don't know how this is going to work out for me.* Karl indicates the door he'd burst through minutes before, and the four of us head through it and down the hall. Martha diverts to the kitchen to prepare tea for me. *Karl has probably already made me a cup.* Karl stops at the door to the control room and turns to face us.

"Jane, I'm going to let Jack get you all settled in. I'm not sure how much of the process he's explained to you already...?"

She glances at me. "Not much, actually."

Karl glares kindheartedly at me. "Typical." *He's being much more flamboyant than usual. Maybe to make Jane comfortable? His way of joking around with her?* "Well, the short version is that *I* will be in this room here, the control room." He indicates the small plastic official-looking sign on the door that says, in neutral inch-high letters: "CONTROL ROOM".

"Oh, is that the control room?" Jane is being nearly as flamboyant as Karl. *Maybe they were always like this and I never noticed.* "I thought it was the 'authorized personnel only' room."

Karl chuckles. "That too." He wags a finger at Jane. "So—not for you!" He gestures with an open hand to the door further down the hall. "You'll be in that room right there, number one. Jack is going to take you there now, and—" he fixes me with a serious-looking stare, but I can see the corners of his mouth twitching, his smile only barely contained. He turns his face back to Jane. "I'm *sure* he's going to explain the process to you, *properly*." He angles his head at me, and I nod soberly. "O.K., so I'll be here in the control room, and Jack is going to get you settled in. He'll explain everything to you in a minute, but once you're settled in, he's going to come back here with me, and you'll be alone in the room. Don't worry— it's quite comfortable, and you can speak to us at any time. There's a microphone in your room."

"I thought you wanted me to explain everything?"

Karl looks at me in mock disapproval. "I *did* want you to explain everything, preferably in advance, so the young lady—" he bows his head in Jane's direction, "so the young lady will have *some* idea what to expect when she gets here. However, we will all have to *content ourselves* with you explaining the process, well... now, it seems." He turns to Jane and takes her hand, kisses it. *He's really hamming it up today.* "My lady, as I said, I will be here in the control room, and I will be able to hear every word you say. It *is* quite comfortable, but if you need *any*thing, anything at all, you just mention it, and we *will* take care of it." He raises his eyebrows at Jane. "O.K. for now, love?"

Jane smiles. "Better than O.K." She takes my hand, unexpectedly. "I know I'm in good hands here." She's rubbing my hand, held in hers, with her other hand; she turns and smiles briefly at me while doing so. She turns her head back to Karl. "With both of you."

Karl nods, glances at me and back at Jane, and nods again. "Good." He lowers his voice. "You *are* in good hands, Jane." *No more trace of the flamboyance, now.* "Maybe Jack didn't explain everything, but one thing I can tell you is—we are very good at what we do. We have—let's just say, a fairly top-shelf clientele."

"Oh, really?" Jane glances at me. "Well— evidently..."

Karl grins and nods his head, almost bowing, at Jane. "Touché, my dear, touché." He claps me on the shoulder. "O.K., buddy, seriously though, make sure you cover all the essentials, O.K.?"

I half-smile, half-frown at Karl. "Of course, man." *Jane is still holding my hand, covering it with her other hand.*

"O.K., then, I'll leave you two to it. See you in a min. Jane—you're gonna do great."

"Thanks, Karl." He leans over and kisses her cheek and then disappears into the control room.

We both watch the door close, and I turn to face Jane. "Shall we?" I gesture with my free hand down the hall, towards the lab rooms.

Jane smiles. "Let's!" She takes off skipping, still holding my hand with one of hers, pulling me along. She pulls up short in front of the next doorway; it has a large numeral "1" at eye-level, and the word "Room" in small block letters above it. "Oh—this is it, isn't it?"

I smile. "That's right."

"Oh!" Jane makes a face. *I think she is embarrassed about stopping short her skipping after barely two skips.* "I forgot it was the first one." She looks at me.

"Well—I was kind of enjoying the skipping. Do you—would you like to skip together to the far end of the hall, and back?"

She levels her gaze at me. "Really?" She cocks her head. "Are you serious?"

"Yeah." I yank her hand. "Let's go!" I start off *skipping through the sunflowers before falling among them* down the hall, this time dragging Jane, but only for a moment, before she is skipping alongside me. We get to the far end of the hall, some thirty feet away, and we both reach out, tag the wall, and start skipping back. By the time we get back to the sober-looking "Room 1" we are both laughing.

Chapter 20

We enter Room 1, and I hold aside the thick dark blackout curtain immediately inside the door; Jane enters ahead of me, and I close the door softly. Jane turns and looks at me. "It has a mechanism so that it opens and closes as close to silently as possible." I smile. "We don't want you to be on the verge of a huge breakthrough and then startle you out of it because someone is bringing you tea that you long since forgot you needed, or something." I frown. "I mean, it's really kind of over—ah, kind of over-doing it a bit. 99 and 44 one-hundredths percent of the time, no one enters or exits during a session. Still..."

Jane is nodding seriously at me. The dim, spare, room, the heavy blackout curtain, the large dark-colored bed—all of it contributes to a quiet mood, intentionally, and all traces of our skipping laughter have vanished from both of us. Jane steps slowly towards the large bed occupying the center of the room. She turns and raises an eyebrow at me. "This is for me, I presume?"

I nod. "Yes. You can sit down if you like. Here—" I reach out to her. "I can take your —your jacket and things, if you like." Jane hands me the light jacket she'd been wearing, and I suddenly realize I'm still wearing my wool pea coat, and I am fairly warm. I hang Jane's jacket on a hanger in a small alcove near the door, and place her small bag on the shelf there. "Oh, so, you know Karl, for all his joking, is right, in that I probably should have explained a bit more about the process before—well, before you got here." Jane is looking expectantly at me when I turn around to face her. She's still standing by the bed. "Oh, you can go ahead and sit down. Make yourself comfortable."

Jane sits and immediately reacts. "Oh! It's a water bed..." She'd sat down somewhat diffidently, but now she flings herself back into the center of the bed, arms and legs spread, enjoying the feeling. She rolls her head sideways to look at me. "I didn't even know they still made these!"

I smile. "Yes, well..." I sit gingerly on the edge of the bed, and she flops over next to me and puts her hand on my thigh. "The idea is that we want you to be as comfortable as possible, but there's also a notional aspect to it, about the idea of

212

water." Jane is nodding and lightly stroking my thigh. *Focus. Keep focused.* "We modeled the process after work done at a meditation research institute, in Virginia, from back in the seventies." *I suppose it's O.K. to be informal with her—it's not like she's a typical client.* Jane's hand is now still on my thigh, and she is lying on her side next to me. I place my hand on her upper arm, and she wriggles her entire body slightly in response. "The basic idea is that we will guide you into a deeply relaxed state, what you might call a meditative state, but it's fine to just think about it as a deeply relaxed state." Jane is looking intently at me, lying on my right on her right side, her head propped up on her right hand, her left hand perched on my right thigh, my right hand having gently moved down her upper arm, across her elbow, and now resting on her hip. We are looking in each others' eyes, she lying there looking up at me, me looking, right, down at her. "The idea of the water bed is, two things. First, the sense of sinking into the water is usually a very relaxing sensation for people. The whole idea, the basic idea anyway, is that you will be very relaxed, and in that very relaxed state, it's easier to —to process things."

213

"Like what?"

"Well, whatever there is to process." She's looking up at me; I've been looking down at her, steadily, my hand unmoving now, resting on her hip in a kind of casual intimacy matching her hand resting on my thigh. "People come to us for all sorts of reasons. Some of them are purely emotional; some of them have more to do with achievements, achievement-type stuff anyway, like goal setting and mentally creating success, things like that. We got a lot of those."

Jane is nodding. "Karl said you have a lot of high-brow clientele."

"Evidently." I smile and squeeze her hip gently, and she smiles and squeezes my thigh. "But of course, you can imagine, business types, go-getters, that kind of thing. But we get all manner. Those may be, well," I pause and look away. "Probably half, or more than half, I'm not sure." I look back at Jane. *Delicately.* I lower my voice. "We have a lot of experience working with clients who are experiencing physical manifestations."

Jane sits up a little bit. "*That*, Jack, is a very polite way of saying people with health issues."

I tilt my head in acknowledgment. "Well, I don't think I have to tell you that the body reflects the mind to a larger extent than most people realize. Bruce Lipton has written about this extensively. He calls it the 'expectation effect', as opposed to the 'placebo effect'. The idea that expecting to get well goes a long way, if not all the way, in making a person well."

Jane is nodding. "I read his book, 'The Biology of Belief', when I was first diagnosed."

I am watching her face. *She really is a lovely woman. She was always lovely. I had such a hard time thinking about her, about her face. For the last couple years there were times I didn't even want to look at her.* "That's good." I reach up and brush a lank of her short hair away from her face, behind her ear. "That's very good, actually." She closed her eyes for a moment when I brushed her hair back, and now she's looking up at me again. "Where was I?"

"You were saying about how it's modeled after—something about Virginia?"

"Yes, well, yes and no. I mean, we modeled our process after a process conducted at this institute, that studies things like altered states of consciousness, back in the seventies. What they do now is different, but we based what we do here on some of their original research. You don't really need to worry about all that. The basic idea is that you're going to lay down on this bed —"

Jane flops back onto her back and spreads her arms. "Done!"

I smile. Her movement dislodged my hand from her hip, and I find that now it is my hand resting on her thigh. "Good. So I'm going to have you put on a pair of headphones."

"Headphones?"

"Yes. They're stereo headphones, and we'll be playing special audio tones through them. You won't really be able to hear them, because we play them underneath pink noise." Jane is giving me a quizzical look. "Pink noise is like white noise, but it has a softer sound to it. Less of a hissing sound than white noise."

She nods and lays her head back on the bed, staring at the black ceiling. "What's that?"

I glance up. "Yes, I was getting to that. After you're comfortable in the bed and have your stereo headphones on, I'm going to lower that microphone—that's a microphone, sorry, I didn't actually answer. It's a microphone, and I'll lower it down so it's suspended over you, so it can easily pick up anything you say, including if you are whispering or muttering or anything like that."

Jane tilts her head to the side to face me. "You think I'm going to be muttering?" She props herself up on her elbow; the water bed gives her body an undulating motion which propagates gently to me. "I think, sir, that between the two of us, *you* are the one that is most likely to *mutter*."

I smile and close my eyes for a second. *Jenny in her bikini staring at me on the beach at Cape May when I look up and she laughs.* I look down at Jane. "You may be right."

She flops back down, undulating me again. "I *am* right." She tilts her face towards me. "Continue..."

I cross my leg under myself and turn so I'm facing her. I take a deep breath. *Where was I?* "The idea is, that when you're very relaxed, and you're speaking, that you may —oftentimes, people will speak much more softly than normal, so—"

"Or mutter?"

I nod and smile. "Yes, or mutter. You'd be surprised, actually, if you listen to the recordings. I know that I am always surprised, because to myself it sounds like I'm speaking normally, but what the microphone picks up is very different."

Jane is nodding. She's put her hands under her head, and I lean almost over her to reach a pillow. "Here, you can put this under your head if you like."

She turns to see the pillow and then lifts her head, hands and all, as though she's doing a crunch. I tuck the pillow under her head and she relaxes back down onto it with an audible sigh. "Mmm. That's nice." Her eyes are closed.

218

I see that she's already starting to feel relaxed, and so I carefully stand up and retrieve the headphones from where they are hanging on their little hook on the wall. Turning around, the bed, as large as it is in the small room, is only a step away, and I stand over Jane. Softly, "Jane, you can keep your eyes closed. I'm just going to place these headphones over your head, O.K.?" She makes a soft affirmative sound, and I lean closer to her. "You might want to brush your hair behind your ears." She slowly removes her hands from behind her head and brushes her hair on either side behind her ears. "Here." I bring her hands up to grasp the sides of the large cushioned headphones, and guide her, holding the headphones, to seat them on her head. "How's that?"

"Mmm hmm." She wriggles her body and slowly moves her hands down to her sides. "It's good."

"O.K." I move to the wall to the control for lowering the microphone, and I lower it and adjust its position to be a couple feet above Jane's mouth. I step next to the bed and squat down so my mouth is close to her head. I speak in the tone I use when speaking to someone wearing big

219

cushioned headphones: not loud, because I don't want to disturb her, but in a way that projects my voice effectively. "Jane, two things."

"Yeah, Jackie?"

I shiver. "First, I forgot to ask you to turn your cellphone on airplane mode. This room is electrically shielded, and we try to minimize any possible interference...."

Jane shakes her head gently, drowsily. "No, I left it in my car. It's O.K."

"Oh, excellent." I move around the side of the bed. "I'm just going to place this light blanket over you. Feel free to move it on you more or off you. Sometimes we feel temperature shifts during the process; it's all very normal, and we want you to be comfortable. Don't worry about whether moving around, like to move the blanket— don't worry about it disturbing your relaxed state. The special audio tones will take care of everything for you. They are designed to hold you in a relaxed state by adjusting your brain waves, so if you need to throw off the blanket or pull it closer, just go ahead and do so. Same thing goes if you have an itch, or you want to move to a more comfortable position. Just be comfortable. If you have an itch, go ahead and scratch it, and then let the audio tones gently bring you back to the relaxed state. O.K.?" I've placed the light blanket over her, and my hand is resting on her upper arm, near her shoulder.

"Mmmm. Yes, thank you. I'm very comfortable already."

"O.K." I trace my fingers softly down her arm until I reach her hand, under the blanket. I feel for her fingers, and she takes my hand, the thin fabric of the blanket between us. I squeeze her hand, and she squeezes back. "I'm going to go into the control room now, and in just a moment, you'll hear me speaking to you through the headphones, O.K.?"

"Jack..." her voice is soft, relaxed. *The tones have been relaxing her since I put the headphones on. It's the preliminary process.*

"Yeah?"

"You didn't tell me..." her voice trails off.

"Didn't tell you what?"

Jane sighs and makes a soft mewing sound, like a cat sleeping in the sun. She squeezes my hand again. "You didn't tell me...the other reason you use a water bed..."

I smile and squeeze her hand. "I'll tell you what—I'll tell you in just a minute, when I get to the control room. O.K.?"

She smiles sleepily, and I squeeze her hand one more time, then withdraw, tracing my fingers over her hand and up her arm to her shoulder. I close my eyes for a moment, and then I lean over and kiss her forehead. She makes a small noise, and I turn to the curtain over the door. I take a moment, gazing at my former wife lying until the thin blanket on the big waterbed in the dim black room, and then I shut off the lights and carefully slide behind the heavy dark blackout curtain, and exit into the suddenly much-too-bright hallway.

Chapter 21

"Took you long enough." Karl doesn't glance at me when I step into the control room and close the door. I take a step forward and he suddenly turns his entire chair towards me. "I thought maybe I was going to have to go in there and break something up. Busy, were you? Making sure the 'special client' gets especially comfortable?" Karl is almost leering at me, but I know he means it good-heartedly.

I shake my head. "No, just..." I shrug and walk past Karl to my chair, sit down and pull the chair up to the table with the controls. "Just..." I realize I'm staring blankly, and I turn towards Karl.

His face shifts immediately *struck by my silent manner probably* and he straightens up. "Hey, man..." He falters for a moment, and then leans forward and claps his hand on my thigh, just above the knee. "You know I'm just playing with you."

I look at Karl, at his face. *In a half hour, I'll know for sure how close we are.* I shake my head and lay my hand over his on my leg. "No, no... I know." I glance away, and then turn my chair to face the controls. Karl makes a sound and I turn towards him; he's holding my large mug of tea. *Green tea, two tea bags. God, I love this man. I really hope he doesn't freak out.* "Hey. Hey, thanks man." I take the over-sized mug and set it near me on the table, off to the side of my binder with the checklist. I take the binder and open to my checklist, and start checking things off. I glance over at Karl and catch him glancing at me. "You alright man? You're awfully quiet over there."

"Man, I was literally just about to say the exact same thing to you. Are *you* O.K.?" He scootches his chair closer to me. "Seriously, man, anything there for you? I mean, it's your ex—your former wife, man. Anything you want to get clear about before we start?"

I glance down at my checklist, then over to Karl. "Yes, actually, but I'm not there yet."

"What? Let me see that thing?" *I know as well as he does that getting clear with someone about anything on your mind is the very first thing on the list. Karl even made it number zero, because it is the foundation of everything else.*

"O.K." I set the binder on the counter, and turn my chair to face Karl. *Maybe some tea.* I reach across myself to retrieve the large mug of tea from the table next to where I set the binder, and hold it in my lap in both hands. It is just barely cool enough to hold but still fairly hot, and I focus on the heat entering my hands, to ground myself. My eyes are closed, and when I open them, Karl is looking at me with a neutral, open expression. "You ready?"

"Ready when you are, buddy."

I take a deep breath. "I have a concern." Karl nods, slowly. I look down at my tea. "I have a concern that—there are some things that Jane might bring up, that I expect will almost definitely come up, if not completely definitely..." I trail off and glance up at Karl. He gives a little brisk nod as if to tell me to continue. I swallow and force myself to keep my eyes on his. *Now.* "Karl, I am concerned—I have a concern, that what Jane says—it has to do with me, with us. I have a concern that—" *Jesus, spit it out.* I close my eyes and take a sip of the tea. It's barely cool enough to drink, but the heat in my mouth seems to penetrate and moisten my mouth out of proportion to the tiny slurping sip that I took. "My concern is that when you hear what she has to say, you will —" I swallow. "You will think—differently—about me. In a way that is not good." I stop.

Karl is staring at me. He waits for a moment. "O.K. You have a concern that I may hear something from Jane that will negatively affect how I feel or think about you. Got it." I nod. "Anything else?"

I think for a moment. "Just—the magnitude of what I just said. I'm probably—I may not be being clear about how concerned I am, about—about the magnitude of what—of what she might—what she is probably going to say." *I'm fumbling.*

"You have a concern that Jane is probably going to say something that is fairly significant, that will affect how I think or feel about you. Your concern is serious because the thing she is likely to say is of some magnitude." He pauses. "Is that right?"

"That's right."

"O.K. I got it." He waits another moment. "Anything else?"

I think. "No, that's really all that's there. I mean, I have a concern that I'm able to be effective with her, in the process I mean."

Karl smiles. "I don't think you need to be concerned with that—I've never known you to not be effective, with anyone. But I got it."

I hesitate. *Should I be concerned with the first thing I said?* Karl must see the look on my face, because he claps me on the knee again. "And no, I don't think you need to be concerned with the other thing either, so don't go worming around in that big brain of yours." I smile. "Seriously, though. Anything else, or are you clear?"

"No. No, that's it. I'm clear." I pause. "What about you? Do you have anything?"

"Nope. Well, yes. I had a concern that you might not share with me the completely obvious concern that your former wife, going through the process, might reveal something at least embarrassing if not downright outrageous, that concerns you." He smiles. "But you cleared that up for me. Thanks, buddy!" He gives my thigh above my knee a squeeze in the way he knows tickles me, and I lurch to get my leg out of his grasp, nearly spilling hot tea on myself.

"Hey, watch it!"

He rolls his chair back to its normal position. "Alright, finish up that checklist man. Let's get to it."

I swiftly double check the remaining items, and look up at Karl. He's trying not to look at me, but I can tell he's smiling. I realize that I'd gone through the rest of the checklist before Jane arrived, per normal procedure. *But I skipped clearing with Karl.* "Were you just gonna let me go through this whole thing again?"

He smiles and keeps his face on the controls, but glances at me out of the corner of his eye. "I figured you'd notice sooner than you did, to be honest."

I shake my head and put on my headphones. "Ready?"

"Yeah, man, let's do this."

I move the big microphone near to the edge of the counter, and press the large "Talk" button on its base. "Jane, it's Jack. Can you hear me alright?"

Chapter 22

Jane's voice is clear in my headphone. "I can hear you just fine, Jack."

"O.K. good. Are you comfortable?"

"Yes, quite. Thank you."

"O.K. good. We are just about ready here."

"Jackie?"

"Yes?"

"You didn't tell me the other thing about the water bed?"

I smile. *Mind like a vice when it comes to remembering things. That will probably help the process for her, once she gets to the proper level.* "That's right, I didn't, but I'm about to. Hold tight for just one more moment, O.K.? Go ahead and continue to be comfortable."

"Oh, I am *very* comfortable." She pauses. "Jackie, when you were leaving the room, I felt almost like I was falling asleep, I was so relaxed. Now I feel—well, I still feel very relaxed, but I also feel much more wide-awake, somehow. Is that alright?"

"That's perfect. You're absolutely perfect, Jane." *I hear myself say it.* "That's part of the initial process. Remember I said that the goal is for you to be relaxed in a sort-of meditative state—specifically, a state in which you are relaxed enough so that your mind is open to dealing with the things we're going to be bringing up, in a way that everything flows easily." *I'm a little distracted by her and me and us, and I almost said, "In a way that lowers resistance," but I don't want to program her mind for "resistance", so I must remember to take care with my words. Especially now, especially with Jane.* "In order for everything to flow easily and comfortably, it is also necessary that your mind be awake and alert, while your body is essentially asleep." *The institute in Virginia has a special name for this state, but I don't want to distract her with too many details right now.* "So the initial tones that are going through your headphones are designed to help you go into that state."

"Oh, I didn't realize anything had started yet."

"Yes, remember I said that you won't really hear the tones themselves, just the pink noise. If you listen, you can hear a sound that's a little like an old radio being tuned between channels." I increase the main volume slightly. "Do you hear it?"

"Yes, I hear it now. I think I was hearing it before but I wasn't really paying attention to it."

"Good. That's that 'pink noise' I mentioned. And Jane...?"

"Yes?"

"Here's where I'm going to answer your other question, about the water bed."

"Good. That's good, Jackie." *Her voice is sounding more mellow. I've switched to the next sequence, to begin bringing her down to a deeper level.*

"Listen:" I press a button on my panel, and watch a visual display begin to move; it indicates to me that Jane is hearing the sound of ocean waves. "The sound of ocean waves. Remember, I said that part of the idea behind the water bed was notional, having to do with water?" Jane gives an affirmative sound, soft, but distinct through my headphones. "Part of the process that we have adopted, is to play the sound of ocean surf at the beginning of the session. The sound of the ocean waves is symbolic of the powerful waves of vibrational energy that flow through all of us, and throughout the world, all the time. During the process, we are tapping in to this powerful, ever-present energy, and we are going to use it to help you, to help you to help yourself. The water in the water bed, we see as a conduit, that helps you to be a part of the flow of the ocean waves, and as part of that conduit, you yourself will be learning to direct and control that flow. Feel yourself now, connecting to the sound of the ocean waves, connecting also to the water underneath you right now. You are part of the flow of energy, the powerful flow of energy that flows through you and around you, and you are part of that powerful current, and with our help, you are now going to harness that power with your conscious mind. Are you ready?"

Jane makes a sound but I have just moved to adjust my headphones, and the sound of my movement against my head has muffled her voice, so that I don't understand it. I release the "push to talk" button on the large microphone with my other hand, and quickly point my mouth towards Karl. "Did you catch that?"

"Cool. She said, 'Cool,' man."

I smile. *Cool, indeed.* I press the "talk" button again. "Cool, indeed, Jane. Let's begin."

***

It's a couple hours later, and I'm again standing outside the building, leaning on a car, only this time it's Jane's car, not mine. I've just walked her out to her car after the session. Her eyes are shining. She was quiet at first, coming out of the process, as people usually are, *it takes a while for the mind to get re-grounded into the regular physical world after being "out there" for a while* but after we sat for a little while and she drank some green tea, she began to open up more, and she has been talking almost continuously for ten minutes.

She's just paused, and is looking off in the distance, beyond me and her car, and then she refocuses on me. "Jack—tell me if this is strange or crazy, but..." She closes her eyes and takes a deep breath, inhaling deeply, seeming to really take the breath in deliberately, and exhaling a long slow deliberate exhale. "I feel almost as though..." Her eyes are still closed, and she opens them. "You know I told you I'd been through chemo, and everything, and that my latest tests showed that I—the tests didn't detect any cancer. I told you all that, about my hair and all." She reaches up and twists a piece of her hair, tucking it behind her ear, which it is just long enough to reach. I nod. "Well, I don't know if I told you or not—I don't think I did, but maybe I did, or maybe—maybe you, I don't know, figured it out or something already, from what I did say or what I didn't say, before."

I'm watching her eyes, but I'm watching her mouth also, and her eyes. I smile, gently. "Well, I suppose I don't know yet. What is it?"

Jane smiles. "It's just that... When I got my results back, they said that they didn't detect any cancer, which of course is what I wanted to hear, but I felt—I *felt*, somehow, that I was—I don't know, still in danger, I guess. Like I wasn't really out of the woods yet. I tried to tell myself that I was just being paranoid or worrisome, or something like that, but I kept feeling like there was still *something* there." She pauses; she's not smiling now, but looking at me, intently. "I mean, really, that's why I wrote to you. I finally realized that, or I mean I thought that what was going on was that I was still, you know—holding on to things. To *things*, you know, *those* things." She's looking pointedly at me, and I nod slowly. "I know you understand." She closes her eyes and takes another deep, slow breath. I wait, watching her, watching her chest expand and shoulders lift, then drop down as her chest contracts; I can't see, but I can imagine her abdomen tightening as she presses the last bit of air from her lungs. *Because I just told her—programmed her really—to do this kind of breath, any time, for cleansing. I can practically trace the movement of each part of her breath.* I push the other image out of my mind. She opens her eyes and looks at me. "Jack, is it crazy? I mean, this is exactly what I hoped for, so I don't know if I'm just making it up in my mind or something..."

"What is it?"

"I feel like—it's not easy to describe, but I feel like... It's as though, when I think about my body, like as though I go inside my body and feel, really *feel* the different parts, my cells and my lymph and everything." She's closed her eyes, concentrating; I can almost follow her awareness running through the different parts of her body. "It sounds strange, but I can *feel*... almost like there is an energetic field there, like a force field. Like something out of Star Trek or something, only not hokey like that. It's as though each of my cells has a little force field around itself, to protect itself against cancer—against other things too, not just cancer—and all the little force fields are sort of pulsing and operating together, and together they connect and form a larger and larger force field, so that the tissues and the organs and everything, eventually my whole body, is working together, and is *shielded*, is really *shielded*, from the cancer, and from other things too." She opens her eyes. "Am I crazy?"

I hold her gaze steadily. *I can feel my own self energy flowing around the hole where Jenny was.* I swallow and shake my head slowly. "Not at all, Jane." I look at her, squinting slightly in the late afternoon November sun, which is somehow both brighter and softer than I expect. "You know it's not crazy, Jane. You don't really have to ask me. You can *feel* it, directly, can't you?"

236

Jane is nodding rapidly. "Yes, yes. Exactly! I don't know how I can tell, but it's as though —when I got the last test, I felt like, they may not have detected it, but that didn't mean it was completely gone. I mean, I guess I felt like it *was* gone, but that—something was still there. It was like, the potential for it to be there was still there, so they'd wiped out what was there, but not the potential for it. Now..." She closes her eyes; she's not doing the full deep breathing, but I can tell she is connecting with her body still. *This is good. She is really taking it on consciously. This is exactly what we were aiming for.* She opens her eyes suddenly, speaking in a very focused, intent way, looking right into my eyes. "Jack, I get it. It's exactly what I was hoping to get by talking to you, and I had no idea it would be—that you do what you do. It's extraordinary. I was holding on to all those things, and it was leaving an empty space inside me that could then be filled with toxicity, and so they cleared out the surface-level toxicity with their medical toxins, and I went to cleanse my body with being a vegan and all that stuff, but I still had that hole there. But now, it's gone. Instead of a hole, I myself," she suddenly giggles. "*I* am *whole*."

I'm nodding. I open my mouth to speak, but she cuts me off.

"Jackie—" She's actually reached up and put her hand over my half-opened mouth. Her fingers are cool against my lips. I close my mouth and she puts her hand on the side of my face, holding my jaw, firmly, intently. "Jackie, listen to me."

I move my mouth, but nothing comes out at first. *I know exactly what she is going to say.* I clear my throat. "What?" *As if it hasn't been obvious for five years, since Karl and I started this work.*

"Jackie. You have to do this." She's nodding as she speaks, her eyes fixed on mine, her head moving up and down slowly, emphatically, her hand gripping the side of my face, holding me in place, looking down at her. "Jackie, I know you haven't let go what happened with—what happened." I take a deep breath, but unfocused; I can feel my chest rising and falling. *Panic breaths. Take control.* I force myself to exhale slowly and deliberately. Something about the focus of the world, my sense of where everything is around me—Jane, her car, the building, the decorative trees, and even the sun melting down beyond Jane's

238

face—shifts, and the closeness of the close objects and the farness of the far objects morph together and waver; it lasts only a moment, but I suddenly feel a reset, a clearing. The air around me looks clearer, sharper, somehow.

I haven't moved my eyes from Jane's, but suddenly, she is more focused in my vision than a moment before. I hear myself speaking. "I know you're right, Jane. It's something I've been avoiding for a long time. I tried to bury it and I blamed you when we were together, but I was really blaming myself and I couldn't, or rather wouldn't, wouldn't deal with it. I need to let this go." *The hole, the empty space in my heart, is burning.*

Jane had been holding my gaze, and now she pulls me toward her, her hand going from my jaw to behind my head, her arms wrapped around me. The motion is so swift that my hands are caught between us and I pull them out and wrap them around her. She's whispering, or speaking quietly, softly but firmly, in my ear. "Jack, go back in there and talk to Karl. Tell him you need to do the process and he needs to help you, because there's something you haven't been letting out. You don't need to tell him

239

what it is, just tell him to take you through it." She pulls back suddenly, holding my face in both her hands. Her hands feel warm on my face now. "Promise me, Jack. Promise me you will go talk to him, right now."

I stare at Jane for a moment, staring *in each other's eyes, lying on the ground in the sunflowers, staring in each others' eyes for an hour or a day, laughing and dancing and falling on the ground and falling asleep and* unblinking, my mind working. Jane squeezes my face, shaking it slightly towards her. "Jack? Promise me."

"O.K." I close my eyes. *Jenny is standing on the dock. She turns to me.* "I'll talk to him about it."

"Promise me you'll do the process. *Today.* Right now."

"I don't know if—"

"I asked Karl if you had any other clients today, and he already told me you didn't. So you're free." She's still holding my face. *I haven't been free in eleven years.* "Promise me."

I nod. "O.K." I reach my hands up and hold her face in my hands. "I promise you. I'll go talk to him right now, and I'll go do it. Right now. O.K.?"

"You promise?"

"I promise."

"You promise you are going to go talk to him right now, and do the process, and let go of—what happened? Of everything?"

I close my eyes. *Jenny is standing at the dock.* "I promise."

Jane slowly lets go of my face, and I let go of hers. She's looking at me. "That's three times you promised." I nod.

She swiftly leans forward, lifts her face and kisses my cheek, in the same motion opening the car door next to me. "Text me afterward. I don't care how late it is. O.K.?"

I nod dumbly and step away from the car. She starts the car up, gives a little wave, and pulls out of the spot. She'd backed in, so she didn't have to back out. *Smart girl.* I turn to face the building. I hear a voice. *Jenny, calling me. "It's time, Jackie."* I walk back into the building.

Chapter 23

Karl is standing in the hallway, leaning on the door of the control room, waiting for me. I've just walked in from the door from the outer office, and now I'm standing still, looking at him, him looking at me, neither of us saying anything. I step forward slowly, passing the door to the little kitchen. Karl is the first to speak. "You look like you have something on your mind, buddy."

I stop walking and close my eyes. I'm trying to remember the details of what Jenny—*no, Jane*—what Jane spoke about during her session, but I can't seem to recall. *How much does he already know?* My eyes are scrunched shut, and Karl's voice startles me. "It's O.K." I feel his hand on my shoulder. "It's O.K." His other hand on my other shoulder, and then he's hugging me, and I'm standing there limply leaning against him. He straightens me up and cuffs me under the chin; I open my eyes. Karl is blurry and I blink and the tears disperse and he's clear. "Do you want to talk about it, or do you just want to go...?"

I nod. I start to speak, but my throat is suddenly dry. I turn my head and cough against the back of my forearm. "Jane said..."

Karl is still holding my other shoulder, having let go with one hand to let me cough. He opens his mouth to speak, but then closes it *realizing something.* He squints at me. "What did Jane say?"

I swallow. *My throat is so dry.* I clear my throat and swallow again. *I've taught myself to not speak about this so much, that my body thinks I can't speak now.* I inhale. "Jane—just now. She made me promise to come in here and talk to you and tell you I need to do the process. Right now, tonight. She made me promise." I can feel my eyes pleading with him. *Pleading to agree or to tell me we can't do it tonight?* My throat feels like there is something caught in it. "Three times."

Karl raises one eyebrow while squinting the other eye. "You want to do the process three times?" He starts to smile. "I mean, if you think that's what it'll take..."

I feel myself smiling; I feel a whooshing downward flowing sensation, as though something that had been filling my body suddenly drained out through my feet. I am abruptly left feeling empty, but not in a bad way—empty in an open way. Karl is smiling at me. *He thinks he already knows what I'm going to say, but he doesn't know the half of it. But it doesn't matter. "It's time," I hear again in Jenny's voice.* "No. No, you— you maniac." I shake my head. "I *promised* her, three times."

Karl opens his eyes wide in mock surprise. "Oh! Well in that case..." His hand still on my shoulder, he turns and pulls me gently along down the hallway, past the control room, towards the other three doors. "It's time, Jack."

I'm walking next to him, his left hand on my right shoulder, down the hallway. I glance sideways at him. *I'm not sure if he just said that or if I imagined her saying it again.* "I guess it's time."

Karl glances over at me. "Do you really have to guess?"

"No. No, I don't."

Karl stops in front of the door marked "Room 2". "We'll put you in room 2. It's all set up. You know what to do. Hit the ready light when you're ready. O.K.?"

I nod and open the door to Room 2.

"You need anything? You alright?"

"Yeah. I just need to hit the can real quick." *Each room has its own private bathroom in the back for just this purpose.*

Karl smiles. "Of course. Anything else, though?"

"No, I'm O.K. I'll be ready in just a minute."

"O.K. I'll have everything ready for you."

"Karl?"

He's turned and started walking back towards the control room; he stops and faces me. "Yeah, man?"

I'm looking at him. My body is tingling, and I feel as though I am rushing forward, though I am standing still. The hole in my chest is burning and swirling, and I keep hearing Jenny's voice in the background of my awareness. *It's been there the whole time.* "Just—" I look down at my hands, turn them over, and look back up at Karl. *I'm awake, right now. This is happening right now.* "Thank you."

Karl smiles, gently. He moves his head slightly. "Of course, man. I got you."

I nod, and walk into Room 2.

***

I'm lying on the water bed in Room 2. I've gone to the little bathroom on the far side of the room. I've emptied my pockets and put my cell phone in the little Faraday cage on the shelf. The thin blanket is pulled up to my chin, the headphones are on, and the dangling microphone is in position. I reach above my head and feel for the old-fashioned metal toggle switch, and switch it to the *on* position. In the control room, a green light has just turned on on Karl's display. Immediately, I hear his voice clearly in my headphones. Jack."

"I'm here." I hear the undulating sound of the ocean waves, and begin to feel my body melting into the water bed below me. "Karl?"

"Yeah, Jack."

I take in a deep breath and let it out. "I need to talk about—my sister."

The only sound from my headphones is the ocean surf, but I know the special tones are underneath. I can feel my mind focusing, rearranging. It seems like a long time passes before I hear Karl's voice. "I know, Jack." There is another long pause, and the sound of the ocean waves is rhythmic, relaxing. I find myself automatically drifting into that special state they refer to as "Mind awake, Body asleep." I haven't done any of the preparatory process, but I have done the process so many times, it is nearly automatic. Karl's voice seems to come out of nowhere. "Jenny." *Jenny!*

I make a sound in my throat, but I don't say anything.

His voice comes again, seemingly from far away, but with almost no pause this time. "Say it, Jack. Tell me that you are going to talk about Jenny."

My eyes are closed, but there are flashes of light and color in my vision. There is a pulsing in the corner of my visual field, a pulsing, flashing. It begins in the bottom right of my field and spreads to the bottom of my entire visual field, arcing from right to left and back, flashes of pulsing darkness and less darkness, with bursts of light. I suspect that my eyes are not fully closed and I've forgotten to turn off something in the room that is casting a light that I'm picking up through my partially closed eyes. I open my eyes fully, but there is no change in what I'm seeing. The room is pitch black. No light, sound, or outside electrical signals come into the room. *Even the headphones and microphone operate accoustically; their electrical connections are outside the wire mesh enclosing the room, making the whole room a giant Faraday cage. Of course it's dark here. This is the process. I'm already in a deep meditative, and I'm getting flashes of imagery.* I close my eyes.

I breath in deeply and exhale in a long, slow, breath, making a sound with my vocal chords: "AUM". The sound fills my body and I can feel my legs and my arms, my forearms, fingers, thighs, calves, and toes, all vibrating with the sound. I exhale fully, sounding the "AUM" until there is no breath left in my body. I repeat several times, and the tingling in my body has merged with the flashing, undulating, bright yet soft lights in my eyes or in my mind. The sound of my chant had filled my skull and in the silence afterwards I notice with a distant part of my mind that the ocean sounds had faded, that there is the pink sound softly hissing, not hissing exactly, but buzzing or purring or *rolling over and through my mind. Jenny's voice, calling me. Standing on the dock, turning towards me. "Jackie!"* I hear a sound, a distinct ringing sound. It's a reminder tone, one I've heard many times before. It's reminding me of my purpose at this point of the exercise. *We call it a beacon, but Karl doesn't need to tell me that. He's reminding me—what? To state my purpose.* I hear myself speaking. "I am going to talk about Jenny. I'm going to go into the part of myself where I have been holding her. I'm going to enter that part of myself, and be with her, and let out what there is to let out." *Jenny is standing on the dock. "Jackie!" And she reaches out her hand, beckoning me. She's standing at the end of the dock, her arm extended beckoning.*

"Good." Karl's voice is steady, calm. It is simultaneously very far away and right in the middle of my head. "You're going to talk about Jenny."

"I'm going to talk about Jenny." *Beckoning me towards her, but I am standing in the sand, and I don't move. She puts her arm down and looks at me.* "I'm going to...." My voice trails off.

"What's there for you, right now?"

"Jenny."

"O.K." *She's watching me, but I don't move.* "What is she doing?"

"She's standing on a dock."

"Good." *She turns around and calls me, "Jackie!" She extends her hand, beckoning me.* "Jack, I want you to go into Focus 21, O.K.?"

Focus 21 is the bridge between the physical world and the non-physical. She's standing on the dock, and I am on the beach, and Karl is telling me to go to her. She has been standing there for eleven years waiting for me. She turns and calls to me, "Jackie!" and raises her hand, beckoning me, and I stand on the beach. I look down at my hands and I can see my hands and the white sand on the ground beneath my feet. It sparkles, and I look up, and Jenny is standing there, watching me. Jenny turns around and calls out to me, "Jackie!" and beckons towards me.

"Are you ready?"

Jenny is watching me. I hear myself say, "Yes. I'm going to Focus 21 now." *Jenny turns around and calls me, "Jackie!", raises her hand and beckons me. The sky behind her and the dock and the sand under my feet, the sand dune behind me though I can't see it, the trees on the other side of the trail, the rocks next to the dock, the cloudless sky and Jenny raises her hand again, and beckons, and without turning around, calls me again. "Jackie! Are you coming?" and everything around me flashes. The sounds in my ears shift, and my body shimmers, and Jenny is holding out her hand.*

"I'm going into Focus 21 now."

"Good. Follow the tones. Relax. You're going into Focus 21 now. Go ahead, Jack."

I step from the beach onto the dock, and Jenny smiles. She starts to run towards me, and disappears.

"*She's gone.*" I hear my voice.

"What happened?"

Chapter 24

Jenny arrived at the beach house a little while after Jane and me; we'd put our things away and were relaxing. We'd agreed that it was too late to go out on the beach, but Jenny suggested that we make a fire. She looks expectantly at me *she knows I love to build a fire, to watch it flicker and dance* and I glance over at Jane. Jane shrugs. "I'm open for absolutely anything."

"Yeah, O.K." I stand up from the couch.

Jenny pops up next to me, excitedly. "Oh, awesome! Let's do it. Do we have wood?"

"We can gather some driftwood. There's always some behind the dunes that's dry enough."

Jenny's eyes twinkle. "Come on, Jackie!"

Jane stands up from the couch. "I'll get some matches and—you guys want snacks?"

Jenny is already at the sliding glass door, and she calls over her shoulder. "Jack wants s'mores."

Jane looks at me. I nod. "Mmm. That's a good idea."

Jane gives me a look. Jenny's already outside and down on the sand, poking around. "Go ahead. I'll get the stuff together for s'mores. You might want to grab the chairs—never mind, just go gather wood with your sister and I'll bring the chairs out."

"Thanks, honey!" I kiss Jane; I mean for it to be a quick kiss, but she grabs the inside of the hem of my shorts and holds me close to her. I feel her tongue in my mouth. *I feel the blood moving, feel myself getting erect.* I pull away after a moment, looking into her eyes.

"Later, Jack." She winks at me, then brushes her hand down against the bulge in my shorts. "We have company right now."

I lick my lips. "No shit. Jesus." I walk to the sliding door and pause, adjusting myself, the crotch of my shorts. Jane is over in the little kitchen, poking through cupboards. She glances at me as I walk out to the little deck. "Hey!"

"Hey!" Jenny is around the side of the house, behind the dunes.

254

***

We're sitting around the fire. Jenny is on my right, and Jane is on my left. It was dusk, or just past, when we got the fire going, and it's dark now. We ate s'mores and talked, and now we're sitting around, gazing at the fire.

"You two..." Jane is looking at Jenny and me. We're sitting next to each other on a large log, five or six feet long. We'd found it on the far side of the dune, and the three of us had carried it over with the thought of putting it in the fire, but I'd sat on it while getting a fire started with the smaller pieces, and had been sitting on it since. At some point Jenny sat next to me, the two of us using it like a bench. Jane is on a low beach chair a few feet away, the chair Jenny had been using on the other side of her, and the chair I never did use across the fire from me. "Two peas in a pod."

Jenny and I look at one another. She giggles and puts her arm around me and leans over and kisses my cheek. I put my arm around her waist and smell her hair. *It smells like sunflowers.* Her hair is bright; reflecting the orangey yellow light from the fire, it looks like it is on fire itself, blowing gently in the slight breeze coming off the water.

"Hey, stay just like that—hold on." Jane fishes in the little bag on the sand by her chair, and pulls out a little disposable camera. "Hold still!" She aims the camera at us. "Say, 'cheese'!"

Jenny and I smile at Jane and say, "cheese!" Jane clicks the camera and then frowns, pulling the camera away from her face and looking at the front of it. "The flash didn't go off."

"You might have to—there may be a switch."

I start to disengage from Jenny and lean forward to show Jane, but she interrupts me briskly. "Hold it—I got it. Don't move!" She raises the camera and advances the film. She lowers the camera and angles it towards the light from the fire. "Shit. It's out of film." She looks up at us. "Oh, well, it's just as well. I don't need a picture of you two looking more in love than Jack and me." She smiles, and Jenny laughs. I look at Jenny, and back at Jane, and I smile.

***

We've put out the fire, and we're inside, and we've gone back and discovered the spare bedroom, full of fishing gear, and no bed. The main bedroom has a king bed which takes up nearly the entire bedroom, and there's a couch in the little living room next to the kitchen. Jenny is standing in the doorway of the spare bedroom, looking at the tackle boxes and the fishing lines. She turns and looks into the little living room, at the couch. "Well, you guys obviously need the bed, I can just sleep on the couch."

"Hey, wait, no. I'll take the couch. You guys can share the bed. I don't mind."

Jenny smiles at me. "You're a sweetheart, Jackie." She kisses my cheek. "But you two should take the bed. It's fine."

Jane is standing in the main bedroom, only feet away from us. She hops on the bed. "Hey, Jenny, c'mon, this is way more comfortable. There's plenty of room!" She's flopped back into the center of the bed. She pats the side of the bed. "Come on, Jack." I follow her over and sit on the bed. "No, lie down. Like this!" She sits up and then dramatically flops back down on the bed. I'm sitting upright; I glance behind me, checking to be sure I won't hit her, and let myself fall backwards. Jane sits up on her elbow and starts patting and rubbing the bed next to her. "C'mon, Jen, come on in, the water's great..."

Jenny is standing at the door. She sets down her bag. "Maybe just for a minute." Jane scoots to the far side of the bed, and Jenny sits down next to me. "Is the coast clear?" Her head is turned towards me.

"Yeah, go for it."

She flops down on the bed, mimicking me, and all three of us laugh. We scrunch around and Jane and Jenny both accuse me of taking up too much space, and they elbow me on either side, jostling and laughing. At some point, Jenny says, "I was only going to stay here for a minute, but you know, this is *way* more comfortable than that old couch." She turns and looks at me. "I may have to take you up on that offer."

"Yeah, right. Offer expired." Jenny punches my arm. "I didn't realize how much more comfortable it was myself." I scoot up and to the head of the bed, in the middle, with Jane on my right and Jenny on my left.

"Jack, you're a beast." Jane is turned on her side, her hand resting on my thigh. "Jenny, honey, you can sleep in here with us. We don't mind. Besides, it's already starting to get cold at night, and this place doesn't have any heat."

Jenny is sitting Indian style next to me. She's looking at Jane, and she looks at me. Jane is slowly rubbing my thigh, and Jenny glances down and quickly back up. "I don't want to—" She stops and swallows. Her voice is quiet. "I don't want to be in the way. You two look pretty comfortable."

"Nonsense." Jane suddenly sits up and leans over my legs towards Jenny. She brushes her hair away from her face, and runs her hand slowly down the side of her face. Her hand pauses a few inches from her chin, and she reaches out to Jenny. "Come here." Jenny leans forward, and Jane reaches out both hands and hugs Jenny, tight. Jenny hugs Jane back, her face on the far side of Jane's head from where I'm laying. "You and Jack are as close as two people can be. You have something that I can't have with him. Which is fine. What I have is different." Jane moves her left hand from around Jenny, laying it on my thigh, up near my crotch. She turns her head and looks at me, and moves her hand to my crotch. She and Jenny pull away from each other slowly. Jane's voice is low, husky. "I can't have what you two have together. I can't be his twin." I know what is about to happen and I close my eyes, but I open them immediately. I feel my blood rushing underneath Jane's hand.

"Jane..."

"Shh..." Jane lifts her free hand from Jenny's shoulder and places a single finger over her lips, shushing her. "I can't share what you two have, but you *can* share what we have." Jane squeezes my crotch when she says this. I'm staring at her finger on Jenny's lips. Jenny's eyes are closed, and I close my eyes. I feel Jane's hand massaging me through the thin material of my shorts, and my body reacting.

I open my eyes as Jane slowly withdraws her finger from over Jenny's mouth, and leans forward. Jenny hesitates, and then leans in towards her, and they are kissing, both of them leaning over my outstretched legs, Jane massaging my stiff member through my shorts. Jenny has her hands on either side of Jane's head. I see her tongue flash and I close my eyes. Jane takes her hand from my crotch. I'm breathing heavily. I hear Jane say, "Here," and then I'm frozen, time is frozen, my eyes are closed but I can feel, I can *feel* the motion of Jane's hand through the air, holding Jenny's hand, leading it split second by split second, my body frozen, my stiffness frozen, my breath caught in my throat, until minutes later, hours later, agonizingly slowly, I feel Jenny's hand being placed on my crotch, placed there by my wife. "Here," she says quietly, and the next thing I hear reverberates in my mind, echoing. "I know you've thought about it."

I open my eyes and Jenny has her hand laid flat against the crotch of my shorts. I can feel the heat of my body reflecting off her hand. She's looking down at her hand, and I'm looking at her hand, and then we both look up at each other at the same time. We both freeze, and then she pulls her hand back, holding it in the air in front of her, unsure what to do with it. I look at Jane, and she's looking at Jenny, focused, intently. Jane licks her upper lip slowly. I close my eyes.

I feel Jane moving, shifting position, and then feel her take the hem of my shorts, sliding her fingers inside the hem, against the skin at my hipbone. I open my eyes and she is leaning over me, her face above my crotch, looking down at it. She slips the fingers of her other hand inside the hem against my other hipbone, the one on Jenny's side. Jenny is watching Jane, her mouth slightly open. Jane pulls the hem of my shorts out and starts to pull them down, but they catch on the end of my erection, and she grasps the hem and lifts it up and out and down, and I've hooked my thumbs in the hem of my shorts in the back, and I'm lifting my butt and helping her slide them off me, and I'm sitting at the head of the bed and my shorts are around my thighs, and Jane is pulling them over my knees and she takes Jenny's hand and moves it to my shorts and Jane and Jenny pull my shorts down over my feet and toss them on the floor. Jenny is looking at my feet and puts her hand on my calf, and Jane has leaned down next to me, kneeling next to my hip, and takes me in her mouth. I shudder and close my eyes, feeling the warmth of her mouth, the wet warmth, and I feel Jenny's hand moving slowly up my calf, over my knee, and slowly, slowly, dragging its way up the inside of my thigh. The pressure of her hand is sending electrical spikes up my legs and my breath is coming out in gasps.

Suddenly, the pressure is gone and I open my eyes.

Jane is going down on me, rhythmically lowering her mouth on me and lifting, not releasing me from her mouth. Jenny's hand is on Jane's head, holding her hair, rising and lowering with the motion of Jane's head. She brushes Jane's hair away from her face and Jane takes Jenny's hand, wraps her hand and Jenny's hand around me, and holds Jenny's hand at the base of my erection. She pulls her mouth slowly off of me, and squeezes her hand around Jenny's, and lifts her hand. Jenny is holding me, her hand wet with Jane's spittle, and she's staring down at me. She raises her eyes and looks at me. I open my mouth, and Jenny shakes her head. "Jackie..." She lowers her head, eyes fixed on mine. She closes her eyes, inches away from where she is still clutching me. Her voice is quiet but forceful, heavy. "Don't say anything." She takes me in her mouth.

I'm frozen, gasping, sweating, hot blood throbbing, pulsing in Jenny's mouth. Jane moves up next to me and turns my head, kisses me. I am thinking about how different Jenny's mouth feels compared to Jane's. Jane is quite a bit shorter than

Jenny, but I suddenly realize that her mouth is much larger, physically. Jenny's mouth is smaller, tighter around me. I'm kissing Jane and noticing the details of the feeling of Jenny's mouth on me. I feel Jane's tongue in my mouth, and Jenny's tongue on me. I close my eyes, and Jane pulls away from my mouth, and Jenny lifts her head.

Jane has lifted Jenny's head and is kissing her. She, Jane, abruptly pulls away, and pushes the far side of Jenny's face with her hand, almost cuffing her. Jane leans back and whips off her shirt, reaches behind her to unfasten her bra, tosses both on the floor. Jenny, meanwhile, her face turned towards mine by Jane's hand, crawls slowly on her hands up the bed towards me. She places her hands on either side of my head, and we are looking in each others' eyes. She is moving in slow motion, or she seems to be. Jane starts going down on me again, and again I notice the distinct feeling of her mouth, compared to Jenny's. A moment later, Jenny is kissing me, and I feel how much smaller her mouth is, how her tongue and her lips are thinner than Jane's. Jenny's tongue is in my mouth, and Jane's is on me. I hold my sister and find myself reaching for her shirt, and pulling it up over her back, and she interrupts kissing me, pulls away long enough to pull her shirt over her head, and then lays against me, her mouth pressed against mine, her breasts pressed against my chest.

***

Later, I am lying on my side, and Jane is behind me, nestled against me. I'm facing Jenny, lying on her side. Her eyes are closed. Jane is asleep, and I think Jenny is asleep. None of us have moved in a long time. I close my eyes. I'm lying on my right side now, Jenny on her left, exactly as we fell asleep in the sunflowers, years ago. Jenny's hair smells like sunflowers.

I reach out my hand in the dark, and brush Jenny's hair off of her face. She opens her eyes, and we're looking at each other in the dim light. My hand is holding the side of her head, where I'd brushed her hair back, and she puts her hand on my side, on my ribs. We're both naked, and Jane is naked, asleep behind me. I move my hand down to rest on her hip. We stare at each other for a long time.

Moving together, as if by design, as if we had planned it, working out the details telepathically while silently gazing into each others' eyes, we slowly bring our faces together and kiss, quietly, softly. I see tears in her eyes, and I feel my heart beating. Jenny moves her head down, wriggles her body, pulling on my side, and I pull on her hip, until she is nestled against me, her head on my chest, my nose in her hair. We fall asleep, and it smells like sunflowers.

***

In the morning, waking up, Jenny screws one eye closed, and has one eye half-open. "Good morning." I'm whispering. Jane is asleep still, turned on her back, facing away from me. Jenny has one eye half-open, peering at me.

Her voice is very quiet, lower than a whisper, small. "Good morning, Jackie." She reaches out and puts her hand on the side of my face. I lean forward and kiss her on the mouth. It is a long, slow, purposeful kiss, and when she pulls her mouth away, she bites my bottom lip. I take in a breath.

I close my eyes. My heart is beating hard in my chest. I can feel my blood. I swallow. "Jenny..." My eyes are still closed.

"Yes?"

266

I open my eyes. Both her eyes are closed now. "I love you, Jenny."

Jenny doesn't open her eyes. She brings her hand down from the side of my face to the side of my back, under my arm, pulling me against her, pressing her hips against mine, nestling her head in the crook of my shoulder. I feel her breath on my ear. Her voice is quiet. "I love you, too, Jackie." I feel her warm breath on my ear, feel the warmth of our bodies pressed against each other, remember the warmth of the night before. I feel my blood. "No matter what, Jackie." She kisses my neck. "No matter what."

Chapter 25

After we were all awake and up, we didn't mention the night before. All three of us were in a good mood, and were joking and laughing and having a good time. Jenny didn't seem quiet, or upset. Several times, I caught her watching me, and we stared at each other, looking into each others' eyes for a small eternity before turning away, but that was normal for us. We were always doing that, and we were still doing that. I took that to be a good sign.

I kept seeing flashes of the night before, and I would feel a shock go through my body. When Jane told Jenny she knew she had thought about it, she could have been talking about me, or maybe she was, or maybe she was talking to both of us. I found myself watching Jenny, watching her legs, watching her butt, watching the the way the fabric of her shirt would stretch across her breasts. I would close my eyes and feel her breasts pressed against my chest, blink and feel a flash of the warmth of her hips pressed against mine before we fell asleep.

We'd catch eyes and it would all melt away and it was just as it always was, Jenny and me, sharing snippets of eternity, looking at each other and watching, or laughing and joking, all reflections of the same way we always were with each other, myriad interpretations of one shared soul split for some reason between two bodies, endless repetitions of a summer afternoon falling asleep together in a field of sunflowers.

By the end of the day I felt like it was all part of the natural process, that it was somehow inevitable, that what had happened was no different than anything else that happened. I didn't let myself think about what would happen the next time we saw each other, or the next; I just let myself understand, believe, that what had happened was a natural extension of how we loved each other. After Jenny left, Jane said as much, the only thing she said about it. "You know, it was bound to happen. Don't worry about it. It's just a natural expression of how much you two love each other." She kissed me, and tugged on the hem of my shorts, and we made love in the same bed, not twenty-four hours after the three of us had lain there together, and, it turned out, not twenty-four hours before

270

Jenny hanged herself, back in her apartment.

She left a note. It said, "I am with you forever. I love you, no matter what." It wasn't addressed to me, but everyone, every single person who knew either one of us, knew that it was written to me.

***

Jane and I split up three years later. It was three tough years. I never accused Jane, never blamed her for initiating anything. I didn't have to—she blamed herself, and I let her blame herself, even though we both argued about how it wasn't either of our fault. But Jane didn't know that after she fell asleep, Jenny and I kissed, and held each other, and that I could feel myself stiff against her, smelling her hair, smelling the sunflowers, and I knew what Jane might've known, but what Jenny knew, that what happened really was a natural extension of our love for each other, a natural evolution of hours and hours of staring into each others' eyes, staring when we were young but continuing, continuing day after day and year after year, as we both grew and changed and refused to let growing and changing change *us*, until I met Jane and we were separated physically but not psychically, the physical separation acting as a catalyst, emphasizing and underscoring the need we had for each other, the need we had to connect and play and *be*, together. Jane blamed herself, and I let her, even though I argued with her, in my heart I let her, because it was easier to let her blame herself and to pretend to blame her too, while fighting against it, than it was to accept that what happened happened, at least in part, because there wasn't a part of me that didn't accept it and want it to happen. I knew it then, I could feel it while it was happening, and I knew it two weeks later, at her funeral, when I saw Amy and she hugged me, and I felt the same feeling, knowing it was for Jenny and not for Amy, that no one, not Amy, not Jane, and not even Jenny any more, could be who Jenny was to me, in my mind and in my heart and in my dreams—my perfect, inevitably perfect, match. *Two bodies, somehow split, but one soul flickering between them, back and forth, lighting each of us, together. We're lying in the sun, surrounded by sunflowers, gazing into each others' eyes. But Jenny shut her eyes.*

Chapter 26

I'm blinking in the darkness. I can still feel Jenny's breath on my ear, but her words have faded. She's looking at me, red hair flaring out behind her, eyes flashing like they are still lit by the fire, and she is slowly moving away from me. The dock is gone, and the beach is gone, and I'm lying in darkness on the waterbed, feeling the warmth of Jenny's breath on my ear starting to fade, listening to the echo of the last words she said to me. "Come see me again soon."

I'm blinking in the dark, and I start to become aware of the high-pitch tones coming through the headphones. It's still perfectly black in the room. "Karl?"

"I'm here."

"Can you bring up the lights?"

The darkness blinks and the dim lights come up. I'm lying on the waterbed, and I can make out the microphone hovering above me.

"How do you feel?"

I love you, Jackie. No matter what. I move my eyes around the room. I start to sit up, but the effort to push myself up on the water bed seems overwhelming, and I let myself lay back down. "Karl?"

"Yeah?"

"Did I—did I answer you?"

I can hear Karl chuckling. "Not yet, but don't worry. You were in pretty deep. It may take a bit to get grounded. Take your time."

I'm with you. I'm always with you. I see a flash of Jenny's face. *You don't have to shut me out, now, Jackie. I've always been here. It's O.K. I know you had a harder time with me leaving... It was harder for you than it was for me.* I shake my head.

"Can you bring the lights up more, the regular lights?"

"How much?"

"Fifty percent, please."

274

A soft light fills the room. I'm starting to feel more awake. I take a deep breath. "You're doing fine, buddy. Take your time."

I nod. "Karl?"

"Jack?"

"You asked how I feel."

I can hear Karl chuckle again. "Yes, I did. About five minutes ago." I glance at my watch, but I'd put it in the little Faraday box on the shelf.

I close my eyes in the soft, warm light. *Jenny's hand on my cheek. With me, always.* I open my eyes; I sit up and swing my legs over to the side of the bed. I stretch. I take a deep breath. "I feel good, actually."

There is a soft rustle, and Karl is emerging from behind the blackout curtain. "Yeah?"

I remove my headphones and place them on the little hook on the wall above the bed. Karl presses the switch to retract the microphone, then sits next to me on the edge of the water bed. A ripple, a wave flows under the surface of the bed, from him to me. I look at him. Flashes of our session pop into my mind. "Karl..."

He holds up his hand. "Jack, it's O.K." I'm looking at him. "Really, it's O.K." He puts his hand on my shoulder. "*You* are O.K." He pauses. "You know that now, don't you?"

I nod. "I do, actually." I close my eyes. *Jenny jumps off the dock, swims in the water. I sit with my legs dangling in the water. I'm laughing, and she's laughing. She beckons to me. "Come on in, Jackie! The water's fine!"*

I shake my head, laughing. "I have to stay up here for a while, Jenny." She pouts at me, splashes water on my legs, laughs when I look down, thinking that my clothes will get wet, but I'm not wearing clothes. I kick my feet in the water to splash her back, and she laughs and splashes me more. We stop and gaze at each other. "I'll come visit more often. I promise."

"You promise?"

"I promise."

"You promise what?"

"I promise I'll come visit more often, O.K."

"O.K.!" She floats on her back, watching me, water running off of her skin. "Hey, Jackie!"

276

"What?"

"That's three times you promised!" She kicks her feet, splashing me, and I laugh and smile and blink, and she's gone.

Karl is looking at me. "I get it." He nods. "We both felt the same way." He's nodding, and he has his hand on my shoulder. "I didn't think about the future, but she did, and..." My voice trails off. "She didn't want to experience any more separateness." I'm looking at my hands. Karl doesn't say anything.

I close my eyes and take a deep breath. Karl speaks softly. "You don't have to let *her* go, to let *it* go." *She told me the same thing, during the process. The same words. "You don't have to let me go, to let it go."*

I nod. I let out my breath. "I'm letting it go." Karl reaches behind my neck and squeezes, massaging my neck. "I'm letting it go, and I'm not letting *her* go. And that's O.K." I turn my head to face Karl. "Can I ask you something?"

"Of course."

I close my eyes and take another slow breath. "What do I tell Jane? And what do I tell Amy?"

Karl nods and removes his hand from my neck. He leans his elbows on his thighs. "With Jane—tell her the truth." He glances at me. "Tell her that you let yourself blame her, even though you argued with her about it, but that you really do know that it wasn't her fault, and that you're sorry."

"And then what?"

"And then what is whatever happens next, happens next. You two have the chance to discover who you are for each other now that your sister isn't an issue between you."

"But—"

"No."

"No?"

"No." He's sitting up now. "You don't have to get into any more detail than that. There's nothing to discuss. Jenny isn't here any more, not here in the sense that you and Jane need to worry about. She'll never not be *here*." He taps my chest, my heart. "Jane knows that, and you knew that too, even though you tried to imagine something different. Punishing yourself."

I nod. "O.K." *Jenny will always be here.* I'm holding the spot Karl tapped, above my heart. *The empty place is gone. It's not burning any more, it's not missing. The wall I put around my heart is gone, but she never was gone; she was always there.*

Karl waits, letting me think. When I look up at him again, he speaks. "As for Amy..."

"Yeah, what do I tell Amy?"

Karl is looking at me. His face twitches, and the corners of his mouth start to crinkle up into a smile. "You know, for a genius, you are not too smart with women. Do you know that?" He pokes my ribs. "If I know more about women than you do, you really are in trouble."

I push his hand away, good-naturedly. "Yeah, yeah, the divorced guy whose twin sister killed herself is all fucked up about women." He's kept poking at my rib, and I punch his arm, playfully. "Get on with it. What do I tell my other sister?"

"Nothing, you dummy."

"What do you mean, nothing?"

Karl fixes me with a look. "Just go home and give your sister a hug. That's it. Just give her a hug."

I stare at him. "That's it?"

Karl shakes his head. "No, you're right. Go home, give your sister a hug, and tell her that you're sorry that it's taken you so long to realize that you really gave her the short end of the stick, because you barely let yourself have a relationship with her when Jenny was alive, because you and Jenny just focused on each other, and after she died, you felt so fucked up about it, that you built a little wall around your heart, and you didn't let anyone in, not her, not your wife, and least of all yourself."

I blink at him. "I—I should tell her all that?"

Karl smiles. "Yeah, basically, but try to say it nicely, O.K.?"

I look at my hands. I take a deep breath and look back up at Karl. "O.K."

Manufactured by Amazon.ca
Bolton, ON

20276802R00166